MOONSHINE & MISCHIEF

MOONSHINE HOLLOW #4

KATHLEEN BROOKS

Forever Devoted

Forever Hunted

Forever Guarded

Forever Notorious

Forever Ventured

Forever Freed

Forever Saved (coming July/August 2020)

Shadows Landing Series

Saving Shadows

Sunken Shadows

Lasting Shadows

Fierce Shadows

Broken Shadows (coming October 2020)

Women of Power Series

Chosen for Power

Built for Power

Fashioned for Power

Destined for Power

Web of Lies Series

Whispered Lies

Rogue Lies

Shattered Lies

Moonshine Hollow Series

Moonshine & Murder

Moonshine & Malice

Moonshine & Mayhem

Moonshine & Mischief

To my daughter for her participation in the Moonshine Series. It is so much fun talking book ideas with her, and for that, these books hold such a special place in my heart.

PROLOGUE

Jane Farrington took a seat on her deck overlooking the mountains just outside of Asheville, North Carolina and pulled on an old sweatshirt. Her cozy A-frame house sat on the top of a small mountain. Her favorite thing to do after coming home from a long day of work was to sit out on the deck. From there, she could see the night stars shine bright above her and Jane could feel the wind swirling off the treetops below.

The breeze always soothed her as she took in Earth's entertainment. The birds calling, the animals scurrying, and the stars shining was all the entertainment she needed. Jane felt the energy of all the living things around her and it brought her peace.

During the day she worked as a nature guide for a resort in Asheville. She led hiking adventures through the mountains and whitewater rafting down the river. During the winter, she took groups of skiers on cross country trails. The outdoors spoke to her and fed her soul.

Jane liked to think it wasn't just because she was a witch with powers derived from Earth, but something even deeper

—a connection to the Goddess herself. She came from one of the oldest family lines of the Claritase. The Claritase were the female witches empowered by the original Goddess herself thousands of years ago to help Earth as humans developed. Witches were given one of the four elemental powers—earth, air, water, and fire—to help fuel their magic. The similarly gifted male group was known as the Tenebris. However, during the past few centuries, the Tenebris had turned from their partners into their enemies. The Tenebris had been hunting Claritase and stealing their powers. What happened to the witches when their powers were stolen? They died.

Jane took a sip of her wine and then a deep breath of fresh night air. She'd been in Asheville for two years. It was time to start moving again. She didn't want to draw the attention of any Tenebris hunters and put her rusty powers to the test.

Jane kept her cover by never using her Earth powers to draw attention to herself, even inside her own home. She moved every two years to prevent people from noticing that she didn't age. Claritase and Tenebris aged incredibly slowly. She didn't look a day over twenty-five even though she was four hundred and fifty years old.

A gentle chime of bells sounded from deep within her bedroom. Jane almost dropped her wine glass in surprise. She hadn't heard that sound in centuries. It signaled an addition to the Claritase history. Jane leapt from her chair, knocking her dinner to the deck, and ran through her open French doors into the bedroom.

"Where is it, where is it," she grumbled as she dropped to her stomach and began yanking storage bins out from under her bed. The chiming grew louder and her unused magic tingled as her fingertips brushed the storage box containing the Claritase book. She pried off the cover and looked down at the ancient book, the one thing she'd managed to take with her the night she lost everything so long ago.

Her finger sparked and the green light of her earth powers shot from her fingertip into the book, unlocking it. The book pages turned to the last page and writing appeared where there had been none before.

The war is over. Zoey Rode fulfilled the prophecy. There are still rogue hunters so be on guard. If you seek safety, come to Moonshine Hollow, Tennessee. More to come as the historians complete the record telling of the battle for our freedom. ~ Grand Mistress Lauren

Alexander had been defeated. The prophecy of a powerful witch joining with her true love to banish evil had come true. Zoey Rode . . . Jane sat back, hardly believing her eyes. She'd heard the Rode family had been killed off. But then again, her line should have been as well. Jane was the last Farrington.

Four hundred years ago when Alexander, the head of the Tenebris, attacked the Claritase under a white flag of truce, Jane had been fifty years old. Her parents had been respected members of both groups although they were extremely introverted. Her father had been a high ranking member of the Tenebris and her mother a high ranking member of the Claritase until she'd married. Yet that hadn't saved them. They perished in the surprise attack meant to garner Alexander enough power to take over the entire world, both human and witches alike.

Her aunt had grabbed Jane and forced her to flee as she screamed at the loss of her parents. After picking up a few supplies in preparation to flee, her aunt locked Jane in the room of the man she was supposed to marry and whispered,

"Your intended will keep you safe," before she disappeared. They weren't true loves. A treaty had formed the arrangement between two powerful families—one neither Jane nor her mother had wanted.

The lock clicked behind her and Jane never saw her aunt again. Her fiancé didn't keep her safe. Instead, he'd come into the room and laughed at her grief and bewilderment. "I only wanted your powers and here you are. Let's get this marriage going."

He reached for her hand and Jane jumped back. "I'll never marry you!" she had yelled in defiance. The memory was still fresh even after four hundred years.

"You will, and I will have the powers that are owed to me in the marriage contract." He'd sneered at her as he'd painfully grabbed her arm.

"You murdered my parents!" Jane had screamed. She'd always been peaceful, calm, and respectful of her powers since her father hadn't wanted her to use them. But she had called on them then and they didn't let her down. Generations of power had flowed through her as she unleashed all she could.

He'd screamed, dropped to his knees, and Jane beat back his powers until he was smoking, literally. But Jane couldn't do it. She couldn't take a life. Instead she had run and she'd been running ever since. But now? Now she could finally stop running.

Jane grabbed the hiking pack she used for a purse and stuffed the Claritase book into it. She hurried to her closet. Chills swept over her when she put her hand on the handle. The hair on her arms stood up and the magic she'd buried deep within herself surged to life.

"Hello my little witch."

Four hundred years and Jane had never forgotten that

voice. She turned slowly, her hands in fists as her power surged forward.

He looked more mature now. Then again, at fifty, she'd looked like a teenager too. Then he'd been a scraggly youth, barely a hundred years old. His hair was still red, but now it was as wild as his eyes. Sadly, he was still handsome. He was muscled and every inch a warrior. He had been the warrior who lured her parents to their death with talks of a truce between the Tenebris and Claritase, but now he was more powerful and Jane needed to be careful.

"You've grown up nice. Maybe marriage to you will be worth it after all." He eyed her as if she was his. He could be kind, passionate, and even sensitive. But it had all been an act to acquire some of her powers—powers her father had signed over when they'd settled on her dowry.

"There is no marriage, Ian. What are you doing here?"

"The war is over and I've come to get my bride, or have you forgotten that we have a contract?"

Jane laughed out loud incredulously. "You led my parents to their slaughter. I'm not marrying you. Ever."

"I will have what's mine, Jane." His voice lowered as he took a threatening step toward her. "I was being nice by offering marriage. But if you won't play nice, I'll just take what I want."

Jane knew what that meant. She'd either marry him or he'd kill her and take her powers through battle. Ian reached up to touch her and Jane lost control. Her green earth powers shot from her fingers and into Ian, sending him flying backward. The tattoo on his neck of circular swords with a drop of blood in the center started to shine brightly as Jane fired her powers at him. If she killed him, the circle would flash and turn him to smoke. And then his powers would be hers.

However, Ian was more powerful than he'd been centuries before. When he fired back, the power slammed into her, chasing her powers back. Jane's fight or flight instincts kicked in as her rusty powers woke. She felt the tidal wave of her powers hit hard as they shot from her fingers and stopped Ian's attack. The second his magical assault stopped, Jane was leaping from the second story balcony.

She hit a pine tree limb hard but it gave way, bending to her weight until she could drop to the next branch. Energy zapped the branch and suddenly Jane was falling the last four feet. She landed on her feet and looked up to see Ian aiming his hands at her. Jane grabbed hold of her backpack straps over her shoulders and ran.

"Jane!"

She never looked back as she jumped fallen trees, splashed through creeks, and climbed mountains. She didn't look back for days as she ran through the mountains for over a hundred and sixty miles while she did her best to cover her trail so Ian couldn't follow. Her legs ached and her power and energy were completely drained as Jane finally stumbled into Moonshine Hollow, Tennessee.

1

THE SUN HAD NOT YET RISEN over the Appalachian Mountains in the sleepy little town of Moonshine Hollow, Tennessee to start the late autumn morning. Zoey Rode-Mathers had snuck out of her small cottage house at five in the morning with her black lab, Chance. She could have *poofed* her way to her small bakery on Main Street, Zoey's Sweet Treats, but she chose to walk through the cold mountain air that seemed to be so clear that everything she saw was enhanced.

Why would she *poof* her way to the bakery and miss out on this? Sure, one of the perks of being an accidental witch was being able to snap her fingers and end up exactly where she imagined. However, Zoey craved normalcy after discovering she'd accidently been turned into a witch by two old women, Agnes and Vilma, and being the powerful key who won the battle between the Claritase and the hunter sector of the Tenebris.

So Zoey enjoyed her quiet morning walks. Chance didn't talk about witch training, battles between good and evil, or the upcoming wedding to the love of her life. A love that just happened to be a sexy, powerful Tenebris witch named Slade.

Zoey flicked her fingers and opened the lock to the back door of her bakery. Chance yipped happily and ran to the chew toy in his dog bed in the corner of her kitchen.

"What do you think about some holiday cheer?" she asked Chance who thumped his tail excitedly. "I think so too. It's twenty-five days until Christmas. I think some chocolate peppermint muffins are just the thing."

"And it's twenty-one days until your wedding."

Zoey screamed and jumped. She turned with her hand on her heart to find Vilma and Agnes standing there. Vilma's white hair was permed in such a style that you were instantly reminded of a poodle. Agnes's white hair was sticking out in every direction since she had decided to grow it out. Zoey gave it three more days until Agnes cut it all off again.

Both women looked to be around eighty. In reality they were closer to a couple of thousand years old. The ruby red velvet tracksuit Vilma sported and the emerald green one Agnes wore hid their age well. So did the magic imparted to them by the Goddess.

"Agnes, Vilma! It's five in the morning. What are you doing here?" Zoey asked as she gathered ingredients for the peppermint muffins.

"Did you not hear us?" Vilma asked.

"Three weeks until not only your wedding, but until the winter solstice. There's not a moment to spare!" Agnes said as Zoey began to measure out the ingredients.

"Can't I just have my mornings to bake in peace? What more is there to possibly plan?" Zoey asked. She turned on the large commercial mixer and turned to the women who had become like grandmothers to her. She crossed her arms and tapped her finger on her opposite elbow in a move that would cause grown men to shrivel when she was an entertainment lawyer in Los Angeles. Agnes and Vilma rolled their eyes.

"Have you decided who is going to walk you down the aisle?" Agnes asked for at least the hundredth time.

Zoey's birth father, Magnus Rode, had left her when she was just a child in order to protect her from the Tenebris who had thought they'd killed the last Rode when they had killed Zoey's grandparents. Zoey hadn't known her birth father was alive until he'd come back in time to help her win the battle against the evil Tenebris leader, Alexander.

The trouble was, during the decades Magnus was in hiding, her stepfather, Dr. Bradley Mathers, had raised her. While Zoey thought her stepfather and mother hadn't loved her because they'd sent her away to boarding school as soon as they could, it turned out they'd done it all to protect her. Her father had given his stamp of approval to Bradley before disappearing. So now she had two fathers who had done everything they could to keep her safe as she grew up.

"Are we talking about the wedding?"

"Oh my Goddess!" Zoey screamed again as she leapt back in surprise. "Would you all stop *poofing* into my kitchen! Use the door. Try this thing called *knocking*."

Grand Mistress Lauren, the head of the Claritase, shrugged one shoulder in her cream boat neck sweater. She used her hand to push her black hair back as she rolled her teal eyes. "I don't *knock*. Now, are we discussing the wedding?"

"Did I hear talk of the wedding?"

Zoey groaned as Grand Master Linus, the newly elected head of the Tenebris, *poofed* into the kitchen.

"Yes!" Lauren said excitedly. "Our first Claritase and

Tenebris wedding in over four hundred years. I can't wait for this royal wedding."

Zoey's eyes widened as she took in the word royal combined with wedding, *her* wedding. "Whoa, whoa, whoa. No one said anything about this being a royal event. We don't have royalty . . . do we?" She was still learning after all.

"Well, no," Lauren conceded. "But if you're going to be negative about this you can leave it to us. We'll plan it all."

"Has everyone forgotten that I'm the bride? That this is *my* wedding?" Can't she just have a simple wedding?

"No, you can't. You and Slade are the symbol of our future."

"Lauren! You promised to stop reading my mind without permission." How was this Zoey's morning already and the sun wasn't even up yet?

"Then you need to learn to protect your thoughts better." Lauren didn't seem to see it the same way Zoey did. "For someone who has been practicing as much as you have been, I see where we need to focus some more effort."

Since Zoey and her father, Magnus, had reunited, the entire witch community had taken them in and was teaching them everything they should have learned as a young witchling. It was supposed to take two hundred years. It had taken them two weeks. It was as if she and her father simply absorbed the knowledge as soon as they were shown it. Now, they were only training with the oldest and most powerful of witches.

Zoey and her father had never received formal training as they had both been born during the wars where Alexander had taken over the Tenebris and used his powers to steal the powers of the Claritase and kill anyone who opposed him. Two of those witches happened to be Zoey's grandparents. But with Slade's help, Zoey's father was saved in infancy and a rebellion was born.

Now, if only Zoey could marry Slade without another rebellion.

"Jane, you look horrible." Slade didn't bother with tact. It took too much time. Jane had shown up in Moonshine Hollow a nervous wreck and hadn't gotten much better in the month since she'd arrived. She hadn't told anyone anything about herself or what she was running from. It was clear she was running from something or someone.

That morning she sat in the sheriff's station with her dark green eyes cloaked in exhaustion. Her curly shoulder length hair was a bit wild. It looked as if she hadn't brushed it after getting up that morning . . . or possibly, that she hadn't been to sleep yet. There were dark circles under her eyes and she seemed to fear both being around people and being alone. She only relaxed when Zoey joined her for walks in the woods.

"Thanks, boss." Jane sighed and took a sip of coffee.

Slade shook his head as he poured himself a cup of coffee. "You know I'm not your boss. You work for the Forestry Department. I work for the town."

Jane just shrugged. "Minor technicality."

Slade looked at the little witch who, even under the heavy weight of whatever happened to her, was still a strong witch. Slade felt the power Jane had hidden deep within herself. When she was this worn down, it was hard for her to control the cloaking she used to hide her powers.

"What can I do for you this morning?" Slade asked, taking a seat behind his desk. Since Zoey went to her bakery so early in the morning, Slade had taken to getting to work before his human secretary got in.

"I found evidence of someone camping in the woods."

"And . . . ?" Slade asked slowly. Camping was pretty big in the area, considering they were in the beautiful Appalachian Mountains.

"This wasn't some one night camping trip." Jane held up her phone to show him the pictures she had taken. "The camp looks abandoned now but it looked to me as if someone was living there for at least a week. The fact that they left it set up makes me wonder if they are coming back."

"I'll look into it, and if I see anything else, I'll pass it along to the forest rangers," Slade told her. Jane nodded, but didn't look relieved. "What's really going on, Jane?"

Jane took a deep breath and Slade could see the battle that was raging behind her eyes. "I'm too tired to deny it. I'm having nightmares every night."

Slade crossed his arms over his chest almost as if he were determined to protect whatever danger was keeping her up at night. "About what?"

Jane shook her head and her whole body seemed to deflate. "I don't remember. I wake up feeling as if I'd been running all night long, but I can't remember why or from what."

"Could it be from whatever you were running from when you showed up here?" Slade asked. He didn't think she'd tell him why she came running through the woods, but it was worth asking.

"I don't know." Jane looked away from him and took a deep breath.

"Why don't you see Zoey? Tell her what's going on. She might be able to help."

Jane shook her head and him. "No. She's too busy learning her magic and planning the wedding."

"She always has times for friends. And Jane," Slade paused. He waited until she looked up at him before he continued. "Zoey and I are your friends."

Jane stood and her lips thinned as she pressed them together. She silently nodded. "I'll think about it. Thank you, Master Slade."

"Just Slade. We're equals here in Moonshine."

Slade watched the little witch walk out of the office with the weight of the world on her shoulders. He hoped she'd trust them enough to share her burden.

2

SHE WAS RUNNING for her life. Jane felt the dried leaves and mud under her bare feet as the darkness closed in around her. She felt the hand of death reaching for her and then there was nothing.

Jane shot up from her bed. Her mouth was open in a scream that was making her throat raw; a scream that seemed to be ripped from her very soul. When she realized the only thing touching her were her sheets tangled about her body she was finally able to stop screaming.

Jane sucked in deep breath after deep breath as her heart rate calmed. Her hands shook as she shoved off the sheets, damp with her sweat. Looking at the clock on her nightstand, she saw it was five in the morning. She'd finally fallen asleep at two. Another night of only a couple of hours of restless sleep.

Jane shoved herself up. Her body felt as if it were drunk from the lack of sleep as she staggered to the bathroom. Tears sprang to her eyes at the feeling of absolute despair as she waited for the shower to heat up. She didn't have a future. She was barely surviving each minute of every day.

And she was desperate. Desperate to know what her nightmares were. Desperate to know if she'd be alive to see tomorrow.

The shower woke her, but not nearly as much as the large cup of coffee did. The shaking in her body slowed as she walked through the dawning light toward Zoey's Sweet Treats Bakery. She'd heard through the local grapevine that Zoey had powers similar to the Goddess herself. That she could see things through a simple touch.

Yesterday Slade had mentioned talking to Zoey, and ever since she woke from her nightmare, she couldn't get it out of her head. It was if a string was connecting her to Zoey and dragging her down the street and to the bakery.

The front of the bakery was dark, but behind the counter was a glowing light. Jane tried the front door, but it was locked so she headed around to the back door. She shivered from the feeling of power coming from the shop.

Jane heard the arguing as she approached the door. Even with the door closed to the cold early morning air, she could make out the words.

"It should be a sleeveless sweetheart neckline!"

"No, the dress should have capped sleeves!"

"I always thought a fur cape looked lovely."

"Laced long sleeves! Haven't you seen any royal wedding, like ever?"

None of the voices were Zoey's.

Jane raised her hand and knocked.

The door was flung open and Zoey's eyes looked wild. "Thank Goddess you're here. Took you long enough."

Zoey grabbed her hand and yanked her into the back of the bakery where Agnes, Vilma, Grand Mistress Lauren, and Grand Master Linus were all leafing through various bridal magazines.

"I'm sorry," Zoey practically sang with a gleeful voice that indicated she was anything but sorry. "But I have a meeting with Jane. Let's pick up the wedding dress talk later."

"Later?" Mistress Lauren gasped incredulously. "Don't you know we are now under three weeks until your wedding?"

"I do." Zoey looked as if she were talking between gritted teeth. "I understand the importance of the wedding and my duty. However, I need a moment alone with Jane. Then I promise to choose a wedding dress."

"Thank Goddess." Mistress Lauren tossed up her hands. "That's all we wanted."

Jane waited for everyone to leave as she anxiously twined her fingers together. Jane opened her mouth to speak when the door shut, but Zoey held up her hand to stop her. The door opened again as Mistress Lauren popped back inside. "You swear you'll pick a wedding dress?"

"Yes." Zoey rolled her eyes. The door closed again and Zoey finally exhaled. "Now we should have a moment alone. I've been waiting for you to come to me."

"You have?" Jane asked as Zoey motioned to a barstool near her prep table.

"Yes. Since I touched you when you first arrived."

Jane watched as Zoey went around mixing ingredients for some kind of pastry that was sure to be delicious.

"I don't tell a lot of people, but I can sometimes see a person's past, present, or future with a touch."

Jane's fingers gripped tightly to each other as fear washed over her—the type of fear that chased her in her nightmares. "What did you see?"

"I was trying *not* to see. I got flashes of you running through the woods and then you were happy."

Jane let out a burst of almost hysterical laughter. "Happy? I can't sleep for the fear, and I'm supposed to be happy?"

"Would you mind if I touched you again? Maybe when I actually concentrate on my power, I can see more."

Jane didn't know if she wanted to know or not. She was there for just that, but did she really want to know her future? Did she want to know when and how she died? Because right now it felt as if everything in her life was careening toward death.

"I don't want to know my future. I just want to know about the nightmares I'm having. I can't see them. I can't remember them. I just want them to stop."

Zoey looked sympathetically at her and then held out her hand. The final decision was up to Jane. Jane stared at Zoey's hand as the last debate was made in her mind. Jane held out her hand and closed her eyes. Fear seeped into every pore of her body as she waited to hear the horrors in her mind.

Zoey's hand closed over Jane's and a warm sensation surrounded her hand and ran up her arm until it reached her head. Her mind seemed to float as something shifted. It was Zoey. She was in her mind. The warmth receded and then Zoey dropped her hand. Jane opened her eyes.

The sadness in Zoey's face told her everything she needed to know. "I'm going to die."

3

JANE DIDN'T WANT to hear it. Instead, she turned away so Zoey couldn't see the pain and fear on her face.

"I'm so sorry, Jane. I know the fear that Ian can strike. I saw that you were to be married to him and that he's come after you again." Zoey placed her hand on Jane's shoulder. Jane felt that warmth again and straightened. She hadn't survived all these centuries by being weak.

"Ian is a toddler throwing a fit because he can't have the toy he wants," Jane said stiffly as she turned around. "When will he kill me?"

"That's the thing," Zoey said, her face marred with confusion. "I didn't see your death, I saw your future. And since you didn't want me to tell you about it, I will be vague. You will be happy. The trouble is when I'm in your mind there are these large black craters. I tried to look into them and it was like looking into a bottomless pit. Those are your nightmares. I'm so sorry. I failed."

Jane saw how upset Zoey was. What was in her nightmares that were so bad her mind buried them so badly?

"I couldn't see into your nightmares, but I did learn how to help," Zoey said, reaching out to her again. "If you trust me."

Jane hadn't trusted anyone in centuries. Zoey didn't know what she was asking. Or maybe she did.

"I trust you. After all, you did say I have some happiness in my future." Jane nodded almost more to herself than to Zoey. She was trying to psych herself up for whatever this trust was going to entail.

"Good!" Zoey smiled brightly and turned back to her prep table. "Can you pass me the chocolate chips?"

Jane spent the next two hours helping with baking and setting up the shop for its opening. "Should I go?" Jane asked when Zoey flipped the sign on the door to read "Open."

"No. Take a seat and let me bring you breakfast after all the help you gave me this morning. Then we need to pay a visit to someone I think can help."

Before Jane could ask more, Zoey was handing her a plate of food and a cup of coffee as the shop filled with the morning rush. Jane talked to the human and non-human residents alike as the morning passed. Polly, a witch, and Maribelle, a human, both stopped to talk to her. They were Zoey's best friends. Jane felt jealous as she watched the townspeople come together. She didn't have friends like that. Even when she was a young witch, she hadn't had many friends.

Her parents had taught her at home rather than sending her to the witch schools. They were wonderful parents and she loved them very much. However, they were over protective. They thought their elite position made them targets for being used for their wealth and power. But then they fell for the biggest con man of all—Ian. He convinced

Jane's father that he was one of them and the only suitor who could protect Jane from the others . . . if he had enough power.

Jane shook her head, trying to erase the bad memories and the fear. Here in Moonshine Hollow she needed to step out of the shadows and become part of the community. She needed to place herself and her trust in others. The first step was talking to the people who stopped by her table. The second was trusting Zoey.

JANE LOOKED at the doctor's office that looked to be from another time—the 1970s to be specific. The lobby was presided over by a woman who looked to be as old as the avocado and burnt orange décor.

"What are we doing here?" Jane asked.

"I had Lauren hire a new doctor. Dr. Thurman fought it at first, but he agreed when she told him he only needs to come into the office once a week." Zoey looked over at the stern looking woman behind the table and lowered her voice. "And it was also contingent on Doris staying on as the secretary."

A green light lit up on Doris's desk and Doris glared at Jane and Zoey. "Dr. Sinclair will see you in room one."

Zoey stood up and began walking back to the exam rooms. "What can this doctor do?" Jane asked again. "You know a human doctor can't do anything to help me."

"Just keep an open mind. Remember I used to be human and look at what I can do."

"You were never fully human," Jane reminded her.

"Yes, but do we know which humans carry a trace of witch blood? I don't. So, you never know who might have that sense to fix things or that sense of right and wrong or that sense of otherworldliness."

Jane thought about it as they walked into the room with the large number one next to it. The one was yellow now, but at some point had probably been white. "Fine. I'll keep an open mind."

The room was similar to the lobby, although the new doctor must have fixed it up some. His diploma hung on the wall as Jane went over to read it. Galen Sinclair graduated with honor from an Ivy League medical school that had been the go-to medical school for centuries.

"Wow. The doc has cleaned this place up," Zoey said, looking around. "The paper on the exam table was usually yellow. And look, current posters. There used to be one for the polio vaccine in here."

"What is a doctor of his caliber doing in Moonshine Hollow? I'd expect to see him in some major city. Did he flunk out of school? Is that why he's here?" Jane asked, looking back at the diploma and doing the math in her head. He was thirty-six years old in human years. Dr. Galen Sinclair was in the prime of his life.

"I saw an article he wrote and told Grand Mistress Lauren she should hire him. I didn't ask how she did it."

Zoey took a seat, picked up a magazine, and gasped. "Oh wow. The magazine is only a week old! The ones in the waiting room are over twenty years old."

Jane didn't know how Zoey could be so relaxed. Jane was a bundle of nerves as she paced around the small exam room. There was a knock at the door, and when it opened, Jane almost stumbled over her own feet in surprise. She knew Dr. Sinclair was young, but she was expecting someone reed thin with balding hair. However, Dr. Galen Sinclair was definitely not any of that. She noticed his shoes first. They were sturdy low hikers from a well known brand. Then she noticed the strong muscular legs, the flat stomach under his button-down shirt, and the wide shoulders. Then she noticed the square jaw, the sexy angles of his face and then the dark brown hair streaked with auburn highlights that seemed to match his eyes.

"Jane?"

"Yes?" Jane said on a sigh and then felt like an idiot. Or more aptly, like a lovestruck teenage girl.

"You forgot to put down your last name on the form, and I'll need your social security or driver's license number." Dr. Sinclair smiled and prepared his pen to write it as she blinked with the familiar panic of trying to remember what fake name was on her license now.

"Um," Jane dug out her wallet and handed him her license after a quick glance to remind herself. "Farrow." He wrote it down and then smiled at her again.

"What seems to be the problem?" Dr. Sinclair motioned for Jane to sit up on the exam table as he stuck the stethoscope into his ears to listen to her heart and lungs.

"Um . . ."

"Your lungs and heart sound good."

"Um . . ." Jane saw Zoey roll her eyes and knew if she didn't tell the doctor, Zoey would. "I'm not sleeping."

"Are you under stress from work?" Dr. Sinclair looked back down at her chart. "You work for the Forestry Department?"

"Yes. That's what keeps me calm. I clear trails and make sure they're marked properly. I also lead education classes."

"So is it you who I have to thank for that new trail up Earnest Mountain?"

Jane smiled widely and nodded. "That was my first trail here. Do you like it? Is it too hard?"

Dr. Sinclair shook his head. "I love it. It's challenging but not so hard you don't want to do it again. The lookout points you created give such stunning views of the valley and the creek below. So, you said it keeps you calm. Calm from what?"

Jane forgot Zoey was in the room as she told Dr. Sinclair about waking up screaming and soaked in sweat. She also told him that she wasn't able to remember the nightmares.

Jane nervously gripped her fingers as she waited for Dr. Sinclair to respond. "You say you wake up screaming. I wonder if you say anything else in your sleep?"

"I . . . I don't know. I live alone."

"Why don't we try a sleep study?" Dr. Sinclair held her eyes and Jane bit her lip. She didn't know what she was dreaming. What if it she spilled her secret about being a witch? Dr. Sinclair was human and from what she's discovered from nosing around in his thoughts, he had no idea witches were real. He was a classically trained doctor; all his thoughts were rooted in fact, logic, and reason as humans knew them.

GALEN WAITED for Jane to reply, but when she didn't he started again. "A sleep study sounds scary, but it's not. I can do it at your house since we don't have a hospital set up here. While you sleep, I monitor your sleep stages to see if I can figure out what's disrupting your sleep. I'll measure your eye movements, oxygen levels, heart rate, your breathing rate, if you snore, and what your body does. Do you sleepwalk? Do you have sleep apnea and the lack of oxygen is causing your body to basically scare you awake? Do you talk in your sleep enough to give some idea about the nature of these nightmares? I can monitor all of that and then we can develop a plan to help get you some good, restful sleep."

Now all Galen had to do was keep his hands to himself. There was something about Jane that drew him to her unlike anything he'd ever felt before. She certainly wasn't plain, although she did look worn down. She was muscular and curvy in all the right places, but a bit too thin. Her hair had these sexy curls that begged him to give them just a little tug as he kissed her, but he was concerned about the strain that showed in her face. Whatever was keeping her from sleeping was taking not only a mental toll on her, but a physical one too. Everything in him wanted to reach out to her and wrap her in his arms. Alas, he didn't.

When Jane didn't answer, he turned to Zoey. What was going on today? Zoey's eyes looked blank, and for a moment she stared at a point on the wall without blinking. Then she shook her head and took a deep breath. "Jane, I think you need to do this. I can stay with you overnight if you'd like."

"You think it's a good idea?" Jane asked, her voice making it very clear that she thought it was a horrible idea.

"I do," Zoey answered immediately.

Jane turned back to him. Her green eyes seemed to plead with him, but plead for what, Galen didn't know.

"Okay. I'll do it. When would you like to do this?" Jane straightened her spine and Galen saw the strong woman who was hidden under the fatigue.

"How is tomorrow night? I'm off the day after tomorrow so I won't have any trouble staying up to monitor you."

Jane nodded and then stood. She held out her hand and he shook it. Warmth seemed to flow through him, but when Jane pulled her hand back the warmth was gone.

"I'll see you tomorrow night then. I get off work at six."

"I'll bring dinner." Galen didn't know why he said that.

He wasn't there for dinner. "To make you more comfortable before we go to bed—*you* go to bed," he immediately corrected.

Smooth Galen. So smooth. She was a patient. He couldn't hit on her. But he could solve her sleep problem, discharge her, and then ask her out for a date. Zoey gave him a wink as she walked by while Jane still looked nervous. "Don't worry. We'll figure this out," he reassured.

"Thank you." He watched as Jane took a deep breath and stood up straighter. "I'm normally very strong, but it feels as if all my energy is being drained."

"I promise. We'll get you back to feeling like yourself in no time."

"Thank you, Dr. Sinclair. I'll see you tomorrow night."

Galen walked them out to the lobby and then watched as Zoey grabbed Jane's hand and practically ran from the clinic.

"Your next appointment is here." Galen turned as Doris snapped. Galen couldn't tell if she was mad at him, the patient, or life in general.

He took the file Doris was holding and smiled at the terrified looking child. "Come with me, please. We'll get your sports physical done in no time. I played rugby in college. Do you know what that is?"

But as Galen talked to the boy, his mind was back with Jane.

4

ZOEY PACED in the sheriff's station as she waited for the rest of their group to pop in. Jane was back at the welcome office at the park's entrance. Slade and his deputy, Samuel, watched her pace back and forth across Slade's closed office.

Slade's human secretary, Chloe, had looked at Zoey with curiosity when she'd stormed in and slammed Slade's door. A moment later, Samuel rushed in. The door opened and Zoey spun to see Chloe stepping aside for Lauren, Linus, Polly, Agnes, Vilma, and Zoey's father, Magnus.

"I am so happy you called," Lauren said as she clapped her hands together. "Let's talk wedding!"

Chloe closed the door and everyone looked excited. Zoey almost felt bad crushing their dreams. "This isn't about the wedding. This is about Jane."

"Oh," was the collective letdown.

"She told me she isn't sleeping, and when I touched her I was able to see some of her past, some of her present, and a little of her future. I saw Ian in her past."

That got a different reaction. Everyone suddenly sat up or stood much straighter.

"I saw her running for her life, but not why. I saw that she'll find love and happiness in her future, but I saw that when I first met her," Zoey finished explaining.

"So, what's the problem?" Agnes asked.

"Besides Ian," Vilma added.

"She's not sleeping," Zoey said as she told them about the nightmares. Lauren and Linus shared a look that spoke volumes. They were worried. "Further, when we were in the doctor's office I got a flash." Zoey took a deep breath. The energy inside her was screaming for release but she had to control it. "I saw blood and death. There were two bodies but their heads were turned away. I couldn't see who they were. I couldn't tell how they died. A feeling of absolute terror washed over me."

"This was what you saw when you touched Jane?" Lauren asked into the quiet room.

Zoey shook her head. "I wasn't touching anyone. It was a vision."

"But what could it mean?" Polly looked around hoping someone could answer it.

"I have a feeling Jane holds that answer."

"I think so too, Slade," Linus told his mentee.

"Could it be Ian?" Magnus asked.

Everyone looked around. No one wanted to think it.

"He's on the run," Samuel said as if laughing it off. "He's alone and no match for us all."

Zoey shook her head. It was so frustrating. "I don't know who or what it is. I just know something very bad is going to happen."

"Could it have happened in the past?" Polly asked optimistically.

"I wish, but the feeling of danger is imminent. I felt Jane's fear from the past. This is different."

"What can we do?" her father asked her.

"I wish I knew. I keep seeing dirt and blood mixed together with dead leaves."

"The forest." Slade understood her frustration and the deep worry she was feeling. She felt his strength when she put her hand on the necklace he'd given her. It allowed them to feel each other's presence and feelings. True love gave them that power, but the Goddess stone in the necklace heightened those feelings. Slade felt exactly what she was feeling and vice versa. "Samuel and I will start daily searches of the forest surrounding Moonshine Hollow."

"I'll help and I'm sure others will too," Polly offered, and soon it was agreed that several of the witches would join the patrol each day.

"Well, now that we have that settled . . ." Lauren started to say. "You said you'd pick one of our wedding dresses."

Zoey couldn't take it anymore. She wanted a simple wedding, out under the stars and full moon with her town surrounding her. That was it. She didn't want to be somebody else's symbol of importance. She just wanted to marry the man she loved more than life.

Zoey reached out and grabbed Polly's hand. The young witch had quickly become one of her best friends. "I didn't say I'd pick one of your dresses. I said I would pick *a* dress. And so I shall." With that she *poofed* Polly and her from the room.

When she blinked again they were in front of Zoey's other best friend's house. "What are we doing?" Polly asked with that bright smile that showed she was always up for anything.

"Grabbing Maribelle and going wedding dress shopping. You have to swear you won't tell anyone else about where we went or what my dress looks like."

Polly clapped her hands together excitedly and quickly agreed before Zoey knocked on her human best friend's door. Really, Polly and Maribelle should be the best friends. They were both eternally optimistic, romantic, and didn't put up with any nonsense. That was the part that vibed with Zoey.

"Zoey! Polly!" Maribelle said with surprise when she opened her door. "Would you like to join me for lunch?"

"No thanks," Zoey answered. She was on the clock until the wedding planners from hell found her. "Do you think you can take the afternoon off? I need a wedding dress and I want you and Polly to help me find it."

Maribelle squealed with excitement. Polly squealed with excitement. And yes, Zoey had to admit they made her smile with excitement too. Maybe that's what best friends were for. To get you out of your own way and enjoy life when you needed it most.

"No problem." Maribelle grabbed her purse by the door and closed it behind her. "I'll just text my boss that I'm having woman problems. Freaks him out. He won't even question it."

"I'll drive," Polly called out.

"Where's your . . .?" Polly snapped her fingers and her car was suddenly parked on the street. Maribelle shook her head. "I was so excited to go wedding dress shopping I didn't even see your car."

"Well ladies, let's find me a wedding dress."

5

POLLY AND MARIBELLE ran off the second they crossed the threshold into the wedding dress shop. They were holding hands, laughing, and gone. Zoey smiled at the assistant and was shown to a room to put all her stuff.

Zoey waited until the assistant was gone before calling her mother. Her mom was in California and with the time difference it would be mid-morning. Zoey hoped she wasn't too busy.

"Good morning, dear!"

"Hi, Mom. What are you doing right now?"

"Just finished getting ready for a brunch I'm going to. Why?"

Zoey had had a turbulent relationship with her human mother until very recently. Zoey had thought her mother hated her and only cared about Zoey's stepfather. Zoey was just a little girl when her mother and stepfather married. Zoey's last name had instantly been changed to Mathers, her stepfather's name. She'd been shipped off to boarding school at a young age and then to college and law school. She'd only recently found out her mother and her stepfather, Bradley, had been working to protect Zoey since she came from an old and very powerful witch family through her dad, Magnus Rode.

Now Zoey and her mother were rebuilding their relationship. Plus, it was really nice not to have to hide her powers. "Can you miss it?"

"Of course. Are you in town?" her mother asked. "I can make an appointment with *the* wedding shop in Beverly Hills if you're interested."

"About that," Zoey said as she closed her eyes and envisioned her mother. "Hold on."

"Zoey, what . . . oh my gosh!"

"Hi, Mom." Zoey hugged her mother who was now looking around the dressing room in amazement.

"How? What? Where am I?" Her mother was clearly flustered.

Zoey wiggled her fingers and grinned. "You're in Tennessee with me, Polly, and Maribelle. We're picking out my wedding dress."

Her mother's shocked face suddenly broke out into laughter. "My, you're learning a lot. I can't wait to tell Bradley. He'll be thrilled at how fast traveling to see you will be now."

"And free." Zoey winked.

Her mother stood up and grabbed Zoey's hand. "Let's find you the most beautiful dress."

THE AFTERNOON FLEW by in a flash of tulle. Zoey achieved the ultimate wedding feeling, second only to walking down the aisle, when she'd looked at herself in *the* dress.

Zoey flashed her mom back home and enjoyed the ride back to Moonshine Hollow with her two best friends. She didn't tell them about the image of blood and the sound of screams she'd heard. No, today was about love, not fear. They could conquer fear with love and they would. So Zoey pushed the visions aside and joined Maribelle in teasing Polly about her crush on Slade's deputy, Samuel.

OF COURSE, it had to rain that afternoon. And not just your run of the mill, regular rain, but an empty the atmosphere's entire water storage all at once on Moonshine Hollow, kind of rain.

Jane had to close the Earnest Creek trail to make sure no hikers slipped and rolled into the creek like she had done when the wind had picked up and her foot slipped in the raging torrent of muddy water racing down the trail. Thanks to her powers, she'd prevented herself from being washed down the cold creek water that was now flowing like rapids over the river rocks from the downpour.

Jane was cold, tired, and a completely water-logged, muddy mess when she sloshed her way to the parking lot. There had been some hunters running for the shelter of their trucks so Jane hadn't been able to *poof* her way home until she had verified with them that everyone in their group was accounted for. After making sure the woods were now free of people, or at least all the vehicles were out of the parking lot, Jane was finally able to get home. There was a clear order from the Grand Mistress and Grand Master that they were not to expose themselves as witches to the humans.

The last engine rumbled off and Jane slogged her way to the small log cabin that served as her office. She walked inside, flipped the sign to closed, and locked the door. After hiding her powers for so long, Jane felt strange drawing on them twice that day. But there was no way she was going to walk home in this.

She cast one last look out the window and assured herself no one could see her when she pictured her bathroom and then *poof,* there she was. She was finally feeling safe when the doorbell rang. Those nightmares had her so on edge that she stumbled back in surprise at the noise and almost fell into her bathtub.

"Get it together, Jane," she muttered to herself as she kicked off her muddy shoes on the tile and sloshed her way to the door in clothes so waterlogged that she left a water trail down the hall.

The bell rang again and Jane slowed to look out the window. It wasn't like Ian would ring the bell, but right now Jane didn't trust anything.

"Jane? Are you there?"

Shoot, shoot, shoot. It was Dr. Sinclair and she looked worse than a drowned rat. Not only that, but the front half of her door was decorative glass. He could now see her standing frozen in her living room. *No magic in front of humans.* Jane could practically hear Grand Mistress Lauren shouting.

"Coming!"

Jane sucked up the embarrassment and trudged to open the door.

"Hi, J-ane," Dr. Sinclair said as paused half way through her name with surprise. "I guess you got caught in the rain. Show me the kitchen and I'll get dinner ready while you get a nice warm shower."

She could die on the spot from embarrassment. "I'll just change real quick."

· · ·

DR. SINCLAIR PUSHED PAST HER, his wide shoulders brushing against hers and suddenly Jane wasn't cold anymore. Heat seemed to infuse her body from that point of contact. She almost jumped back in surprise. She'd never felt anything like it before. However, what she really wanted to do was to lean into it.

"Take a long hot shower. Doctor's orders. I mean it. It'll take me at least forty-five minutes to get dinner ready."

"Ready? I thought you were picking up dinner?" Jane asked as she trailed after him. She watched as he took in her comfortable living room with its over-stuffed furniture. She had a television, but the stack of books on the coffee table was how she liked to relax.

He took a quick look and then continued walking toward the back of her cottage. The living room was open to the dining room behind it with a little four-person table. Behind that were the patio doors leading out back. To the left of the dining room was the open kitchen separated from the two rooms by an L-shaped counter with bar stools on the outside, looking into the kitchen.

"I said I was bringing dinner. I thought I'd make my family's famous Sinclair Stew. I also brought some shortbread cookies I made last night and some nice tea. I promise, you'll be so full you'll have no trouble sleeping tonight. My Nan used to say this food would stick to your ribs, and she was right. You will not be hungry in the middle of the night."

Jane watched as he pulled out a dented round tin from a large bag and opened it up. The second he did, she smelled the sweet shortbread cookies inside. Then he pulled out a container of cubed potatoes, carrots, chunks of meat, and cans of various ingredients. "Do you have a large pot I can borrow? Mine's at home if you don't."

"Yeah, right over there," Jane told him. As soon as he turned around to look, she wiggled her fingers. "Yes, that cabinet."

She felt as if she were crossing her fingers behind her back and hoping to not get caught when using her magic. "This is very nice of you, Dr. Sinclair."

"Please, call me Galen. I'm happy to have someone to cook for. Since moving here I've met a lot of people but haven't made any real friends, and I've been eating alone every night. I know tonight is work, but I look forward to getting to know you too."

Jane was sure there was steam coming off her clothes as her body heated. There was something about Galen Sinclair that spoke to her in every way possible.

"Go shower. I've got this."

"Just shout if you need anything else."

"Will do. Enjoy your shower," Galen called out to her as she tried to hurry down the hall as much as her heavy wet clothes would allow.

6

————

"ENJOY YOUR SHOWER? I'm such an idiot," Galen muttered to himself as he began mixing up the stew his family had made for more generations that Galen could count. He was trying to think of the perfect thing to say for a date, but this wasn't a date. And why was he making his family's special stew and shortbread for a patient? He'd never cooked for any woman in the past. "She's not your girlfriend." Idiot, he told himself again.

The second Galen touched Jane during his exam, he was a goner. He'd thought of nothing else. It was strange. Very strange. He was a man of science and extensive education. He did not believe in love at first sight. Lust? Heck, yes. That was explained by pheromones. *This* was something completely different. It was as if his whole being demanded he be in Jane's presence.

Galen let out a long breath when he heard the shower turn on. It took all he had not to push open the bathroom door and offer to help Jane in the shower. He was like a man possessed. Galen closed his eyes for a second and shook his head as a childhood memory shoved it way to the forefront of his mind.

He had been a young boy. No older than six when his Nan came to visit his family in America. She came every winter to stay for two months and then he'd go spend the summer with her.

The memory played out in the stew he was mixing. The same stew his Nan had been making when she told him of the Legend of the Selkie. They were seals that could shed their skins when on land to appear human. They were both loved and feared. It was said that if a human saw a Selkie without their skin, they would fall madly in love. However, no matter how romantic the story began they all ended in heartbreak.

Sure, they were nothing but old legends, but his Nan had told him to take the warning given in the story. Like with the Selkies, not everything in life was as it seemed.

"WHAT A MISERABLE FREAKING NIGHT." Samuel grumbled for the hundredth time as he trudged next to Slade.

Yes, it was the mother of all thunderstorms and they were sludging through the woods surrounding Moonshine Hollow. Slade would rather be doing anything else, especially if it meant being with his true love. The wedding planning had been weighing heavy on Zoey. No matter how he tried to talk to Grand Mistress Lauren and Grand Master Linus, they were set on it being the wedding of the millennium.

"You know Zoey has been having visions. We need to protect our people," Slade finally responded.

"Does it have to be tonight?" Samuel complained.

"Am I making you miss a hot date?" Slade tried to act innocent in his question, but he knew it would annoy Samuel. Samuel had a crush on Polly, a very cute and sweet fire power witch. The thing was, the Claritase and Tenebris had been separated for so many centuries they didn't know what to do with each other now. Dating was much different hundreds of years ago.

"You know I don't," Samuel snapped. He was a fierce warrior, but not so fierce when it came to gathering the courage to ask Polly out.

"Then stop complaining and let's finish this search. And the reason for doing it tonight was because of the noise of the rain. If there are rogue Tenebris hunters still out here, they wouldn't hear us coming."

Slade was on high alert under the hood of his black raincoat as they marched through the woods. The smell of the rain, the darkness of the woods, and the sinking of his feet in the wet leaves all seemed to heighten Slade's senses.

He didn't know what it was, but something was wrong. Something had the woods quiet, and it wasn't the storm. Every ounce of magic in his body was unsettled.

"Slade!"

Slade began running toward Samuel the second he called out. They had been walking about twenty feet apart while they searched a popular hunting area for humans. Using his flashlight instead of powers, Slade scanned the area.

"Down there," Samuel said with a frown.

Slade lowered the light and cursed. A man lay on the ground in a heavy camouflage jacket. He scanned the area and found the tree stand the hunter had been in. His rifle was still up there.

"Should I call it in?" Samuel asked.

"I don't see a bullet wound," Slade said as he reached into his pocket and pulled out a pair of exam gloves. It took a bit to slip them on, but then he was able to bend down and push the man over to his back.

This time both he and Samuel cursed. This man didn't die of a gunshot or stab wound. He also didn't die from falling out of the tree stand. The electric burn mark on the middle of his head told the two men exactly what had happened and who had done it.

"Tenebris hunter," Samuel said with disbelief. "Zoey was right. There is something bad in the woods."

A COLD CHILL ran down Jane's spine as the hot water washed over her. The feeling was there, but then it was gone—Ian. It had to be. And here she was in the shower daydreaming of the human man in her kitchen. What was wrong with her? She couldn't possibly have a fling with a human right now. Especially not a doctor.

He would notice the abnormal things, like her ability to heal from minor injuries far too quickly. Or the fact that her blood was different from human blood on a molecular level that only the Goddess who created them knew about. In those small differences, the Goddess had empowered the witches their ability to help heal others and to help the then newly emerging human civilization. They had done so for thousands of years. Ancient civilizations had called them healers . . . until the witch trials. Then when former Grand Master Alexander of the Tenebris attacked the Claritase to steal their powers they had been forced farther underground.

It had been so long since Jane had helped a human as

her mother had taught her. She'd healed some sprained ankles of the hikers she led over the years, but it had been so minor they had said it had been the ibuprofen they'd taken. No matter the strange reaction she had when she was around Galen, she had to keep away from him. It wasn't safe for her and it wasn't safe for him.

Jane stepped from the shower with determination. She needed to get tonight over with, recover her memories so she could help the other witches protect themselves from Ian, and never go near Galen Sinclair again.

OH NO. No. No. No.

The image of the man in Jane's kitchen with the sleeves rolled up exposing strong muscular arms as he ladled heaping scoops of stew into big bowls had Jane frozen in place as her heart seemed to reach for him.

Her body warmed and the need to touch Galen was so strong that Jane was already stepping forward before she caught herself.

"Right on time." Galen turned toward her, holding two bowls of stew, and smiled. Oh no. She was lost.

"In my family we drink this with whisky, but I also brought some red wine if you'd like that," Galen told her as he smiled at her. "I'll put this on the table if you want to pour yourself a drink and join me."

Jane took a deep breath. He was a human and there was nothing he could do to her. She was the one who was far superior in every way. She could travel anywhere in the world with a twitch of her finger. She could heal broken bones or restart a heart with a touch of her hands. Surely she was strong enough to fight a base emotion like desire.

"Sure. I haven't had whisky in centuries." Oh, my

Goddess. Jane put on a big smile and hoped Galen thought she was being figurative. Ian had loved whisky and she'd never wanted to so much as touch it after the night of his treason.

She grabbed the bottle and two glasses before joining Galen at the table. Jane decided to drink instead of talk. The first sip went down like a shot of fire. The warmth settled in her belly as her body slowly began to unwind and she took another sip.

Jane noticed that Galen was waiting to eat until she took her first bite. The old and seldom seen gentlemanly manners brought her to a time when there had been castles where men fed their loves from a shared trencher.

Jane took a bite of the stew and felt transported back centuries to a time she spent in one of those castles. She'd been so young, not even fifty years old, when she'd had stew like this at a castle with her parents before visiting a seer of sorts at some powerful standing stones in Scotland. Her parents had been worried she'd be a target and used for her wealth and power, so they were with humans more often than not. That night they had sat among the humans as they ate, drank, and talked. In fact, it was her last happy memory before her life changed.

Then they'd visited the stones and her fate had been sealed. However, with one bite of stew she was brought back to that happy time. It was magical how certain smells and tastes could bring back such specific memories.

"This is wonderful. Thank you. This brought back a very happy memory for me from my childhood."

"I'm glad." Galen smiled kindly at her and Jane knew it wasn't time to relax yet. He'd started with questions about where she was from, if she were an only child, and what did her parents do. They were all standard questions, but she didn't have the standard answers humans expected. Instead, she told him the variation of the truth.

"I'm from England. I went to school in the United States when my parents were killed at an early age, so I don't have an accent now."

"How where they killed?" Leave it up to a doctor to want the medical details.

"In a fire. I was lucky enough to escape." Arson in the form of Ian's fire power.

"I'm so sorry. Do you think your nightmares could have a basis in that trauma?"

Jane took another bite of the stew and let the happy memory of their time in the castle ease her worries for a moment. "I don't know. I guess it could but I don't know why it's started now."

Instead of letting Galen ask more questions, Jane turned the questioning on him. Only it did more to damage her plans to distance herself from him. She loved hearing him talk. She loved the family stories of his tight little family and his quirky Nan.

Dinner was long done and cleaned up as they continued to talk books and then medicine. Ancient knowledge that Jane had learned about the human body awakened slowly as they discussed his work. Galen was an open book and she loved flipping the pages of his life.

"You're all set," he said as he stood up from where he had finished attaching all the required equipment. "I'll be in the living room monitoring everything."

"Thank you for putting me at ease tonight. You never did tell me how you ended up in Moonshine Hollow." Jane snuggled into her bed feeling slightly uncomfortable with the equipment attached, but safer than she had in a long while.

"Let's just say Lauren made me an offer I couldn't refuse. Now it's time for you to get to sleep. Good night, Jane. Thank you for the best night I've had in Moonshine Hollow."

Galen bent down and placed his lips on her cheek. It was over before Jane could even sigh in pleasure at the velvet soft touch of them. When her eyes opened, Galen was already out of the door.

7

STUPID. Stupid. Stupid. It had been five hours and Galen still couldn't believe how stupid he'd been for kissing Jane. She was his patient. He didn't even know her. Well, that wasn't exactly true. He'd just had the best "dinner date" of his life. They'd talked as if they'd been friends forever, even though they were just beginning to learn everything about each other.

Galen stood from the couch and ran his hand over his face. It was one in the morning and he had five more hours to go on the test. She hadn't fallen into REM sleep until twenty minutes ago.

What was he going to do about Jane?

What could he do? Nothing. He had to step back. She was his patient.

"Maybe Dr. Thurman would take her," Galen said to himself as he began to pace. "No, I couldn't do that to her. I care too much to pass her off on him."

Galen stopped pacing. This was nuts. He shouldn't care so much about a woman he just met. But the fact was, he did care. Galen took a deep breath. He was a doctor. He was trained to assess facts dispassionately and used to thinking rationally. What was he feeling and why? Lust caused by pheromones? Yes. But his heart shouldn't feel so engaged if it were just lust. Galen closed his eyes and replayed dinner. He revisited his feelings and put them into categories. Lust, friendship, empathy, love, trust, suspicion.

Galen opened his eyes as that realization hit him hard. Even though there was no reason for it, he was suspicious of Jane. There were dots that couldn't be connected. Times when she'd stiffened. When her answers became vague.

Selkie.

Galen shivered as the voice of his dearly departed Nan echoed as if she were standing right next to him. Selkies were mythological creatures. They certainly weren't real. Galen shook his head and took a deep breath. He glanced at the equipment and saw that Jane's brain functions were going crazy. Her pulse looked as if she were running for her life. Her brain function was as if she were awake and solving the most complex puzzle known to man.

Galen ran from the living room and then slowly pushed open her bedroom door. He watched her rapid eye movements as his own eyes widened. Her eyes were moving so fast that he couldn't keep count.

Galen took a step closer. Not only were her eyes moving, her mouth was too. She was talking.

"No, Ian! I will never give you my power. I'll kill you first!"

Galen almost stumbled backward as Jane shot up from the pillow as she screamed. Galen watched her carefully, she was still deeply asleep yet sitting up in bed. Her hands were outstretched as if she were fighting someone off.

"Don't touch me! I won't you let you do this. I won't let you hurt anyone else."

Galen looked over and made sure the video was recording. He was taping her for the entire night and would show her this in the morning. Her hands shot out in front of her, her fingers clawed. "I'll kill you! I should have done it the last time."

Galen watched as her hands were outstretched. Suddenly the hair on his arms rose as if he'd touched an electrical circuit.

Selkie.

Galen looked around as if he expected to see his dead Nan standing next to him.

Crash!

Galen's head snapped to the side at the sound of the front door being kicked open. What the heck? Galen looked quickly back at Jane, caught in the throes of a night terror, and knew he'd do anything to protect her. He flipped the lock on her bedroom door and closed it behind him.

"Jane."

He heard a male voice call out as he crept forward down the dark hallway. He kept to the shadows as he got close enough to find a man standing there with a hunting rifle held loosely in his hands.

"Jud," Galen said loud and clear. He'd treated this man two days ago in the clinic. Was he Jane's boyfriend? Was that what she was hiding?

Jud was twenty-six, about five feet nine inches tall, and he was a country boy through and through. He was a nice enough kid who worked at the distillery in town.

"What are you doing here?" Galen asked as Jud turned slowly in his direction. He raised the rifle and Galen quickly held up his hand.

"Jane."

"I'm not Jane. It's me, Dr. Sinclair."

"Jane."

Galen took a step closer and realized Jud's eyes were unfocused. It was almost as if he were sleepwalking. Jud cocked his head at Galen and began to walk toward him with his rifle resting loosely once again in his hands.

"Jane."

What the heck?

"Stop, Jud." Galen ordered. He held up his hands, but Jud didn't stop. Galen shoved Jud back. "What do you need Jane for?"

"Get Jane. Get Jane. Get Jane," Jud repeated over and over again, giving Galen the shivers.

Jud shoved back and Galen had to react. He blocked the hallway Jud tried to get down. The force of the hit had Galen dropping down into a Rugby stance. When Jud tried to shove past him again, Galen grabbed Jud's jacket at the man's chest and using the force of his body, surged upward and back. Jud went down with Galen on top of him.

"Get Jane. Get Jane. Get Jane," Jud repeated over and over as Galen and he fought over the rifle. Jud tried to wiggle the rifle free as Galen pinned the barrel down to the ground with his left hand. Galen used the advantage of being on top and sat up, his leg squeezing Jud and holding him in place as Galen pulled his right arm back and brought his fist down hard.

The punch connected and Galen didn't feel the impact. He was holding the rifle down with one hand and was ready to punch again when Jud's eyes rolled back in his head.

What the heck was going on? This had to be a nightmare. Galen kept Jud pinned as he pulled the rifle from his grasp, unloaded it, and then tossed it to the other side of the living room before pulling out his cell phone.

"WHAT THE HELL IS GOING ON?" Slade asked Samuel as they looked at the two men they'd just hauled into the jail.

"Get Jane. Get Jane. Get Jane." Slade could still hear the men chanting from their jail cells.

Slade and Samuel had been taking pictures of the crime scene in the woods as they waited for the medical examiner from a nearby town to arrive. It had taken hours but they'd finally manipulated the medical examiner into saying the hunter had fallen from his tree stand and broken his neck.

It wasn't hard to manipulate humans' thoughts, but it seemed the whole night took forever. The medical examiner's van left and Slade and Samuel were about to leave too when they'd heard boots stomping through the woods.

Whoever had been coming wasn't coming quietly. They were plowing through the woods loud as could be. They'd pushed by Slade and Samuel as if they hadn't been standing there. And that's when the whole situation got weirder.

"This is freaky," Samuel said, looking back toward the jail cells.

"Something isn't right. I'm calling Linus." Slade and the others had agreed to minimize magic around humans, but Slade needed answers. "Sorry to wake you, Grand Master," Slade said into his cell phone. "We have an issue."

Slade explained about the hunters and how when they'd asked the men what they were doing. They'd told Slade and Samuel they were to get Jane. "They haven't stopped saying it. I want permission to go into their minds."

"Are they humans?" Linus asked.

"Yes, sir."

There was a pause and then Linus answered. "Do it. Let me know what you find too."

"Yes, sir."

Slade hung up the phone and turned to Samuel. "Let's see what's going on in there."

Slade was about to walk back toward the cells when his phone rang again. "Change your mind?" Slade asked think it was Linus.

"Sheriff?"

"Yes?" Slade said, pulled the phone back and saw an unfamiliar number on the display.

"This is Galen Sinclair. I'm over at Jane Farrow's house conducting a sleep study and Jud just came in trying to take her."

Slade snapped to get Samuel's attention and put the phone on speaker. "Is Jane safe?"

"Yes. I knocked Jud unconscious and have him pinned. I don't know how long he'll be out."

"I'll be right there," Slade said before ending the call. "The Grand Master gave us permission to root around their minds. Do it. I'll be over at Jane's. Call me when you have something."

8

Slade wasn't surprised to see Zoey waiting outside of Jane's house. "I felt your emotions. What's going on?" His true love knew him as well as he knew himself. Sometimes more since Slade didn't like to acknowledge any emotions beyond love, happiness, and desire.

"Samuel and I stopped two hunters who wanted to get Jane. I don't know exactly what that means, but Dr. Sinclair has another hunter in there who tried to get her as well."

His fiancée shook her head. She looked tired. There were dark circles under her eyes and suddenly Slade felt something else—worry for his true love.

"That must be the woods that I saw in my vision."

"At least we stopped it before there was the blood you saw."

"I hope. Come on, let's check on Jane." Zoey didn't wait for him, but instead bounded up the stairs and knocked on the partially open door.

"It's busted, sweetness," Slade said, giving her a wink as he pushed it open. He took in the large footmark on the door by the knob. It appeared the door was kicked in and then slammed shut. Well, as much as it would shut. "Sheriff's Department," Slade called out.

It didn't take him long to see Dr. Sinclair. He was straddling an unconscious Jud in the hallway. Slade let his eyes scan the area and saw the rifle across the room.

"Where's Jane?" Zoey asked almost frantically.

"She's still sleeping. Let her," Dr. Sinclair answered as he slowly stood up. "There's something going on here that I don't understand."

"Tell me everything," Slade said, knowing he was going to wipe Dr. Sinclair's memory as soon as possible.

Slade listened to Dr. Sinclair as Zoey silently went down the hall and peeked into Jane's room. A second later she was back with a worried look on her face. "Jane is thrashing about the bed as if she's running."

"I would have sworn I locked the door." Dr. Sinclair shook his head. "Whatever grips her in terror at night is dark and dangerous to her mind. She doesn't just dream it. She lives it, over and over again. No wonder she's so worn down. Even though she's asleep, she's not getting rest," Dr. Sinclair told them.

"Slade." Samuel was already there and Slade needed Dr. Sinclair gone.

"One moment, Samuel." Slade turned to Dr. Sinclair and reached into his mind only to meet a wall. What the heck? "Doctor, you will go into the other room and sit until I come get you." Slade laced the command with enough magic to control a group of twenty humans.

"Why would I do that? What's going on?" Galen asked.

Something was definitely wrong here. Was his magic not working? Slade reached out again using his magic and was once again blocked.

"I need a moment with my deputy. Zoey, can you take

Dr. Sinclair into the other room while we talk and get Jud out of here?" Slade asked her as he sent her a look to convey it was important.

"Sure thing. Maybe Dr. Sinclair can tell me more about night terrors." Thankfully Zoey understood and steered Galen down the hall and away from Samuel and Slade.

"Give me a second," Slade told his deputy as he reached out with his magic and entered Jud's mind. "Son of a—" Slade took a deep breath and turned with thinned lips to Samuel. "Did you see him?"

"Yes. Ian is spelling the humans to capture Jane and bring her to him."

"The question is why." Slade looked down at the unconscious man as he placed his hands on his hips. "I'm going to have to tell the council."

"I'll let you have the honor of that. I'll take Jud to jail with the others." Samuel leaned down and hefted Jud up and over his shoulder.

Slade sent out a text. He'd meet with them in ten minutes, but first he needed to get Zoey. Slade headed down the hall. When he heard screaming, Slade burst into a sprint as he ran toward the sound. Zoey's hand was covering her mouth, but it wasn't her screaming. Jane was sitting straight up in bed and looked as if she were being choked. However, there wasn't anyone in bed choking her.

"Wake her up!" Slade demanded but Dr. Sinclair stopped him.

"Quiet. I hate seeing her like this too, but it's necessary for the sleep study. I need to find out how long she's in the grips of these terrors, and I'm hoping she'll say something to indicate what they're about," Dr. Sinclair whispered as he dropped his hand from where he'd gripped Slade's arm.

Slade looked at the doctor and saw that he flinched with each of Jane's screams. "I'm entrusting you with her care."

"I'll protect her with my life," Galen swore, and Slade believed him.

"I know you will. I've already seen evidence of it. I need you to stay with her. There are other threats, and we have to get to the bottom of them. Call me when she wakes or if you need anything at all. No matter the time."

"I will."

Slade held out his hand and Zoey immediately placed hers in his. They didn't talk again until they were outside.

"What is going on, Slade?" Zoey finally asked.

"Ian is sending humans to get Jane. They didn't say, 'kill' so I think he wants her for some reason."

"Is all this because she was engaged to him?"

Slade stopped dead in his tracks. "What?"

"Before the war. She was engaged to him against her will."

"Why didn't you tell me this?" Slade asked as he began to run down the sidewalk, dragging her behind him. He needed to get to Lauren's house and luckily it was only a couple blocks over.

"It was so long ago I didn't know how it could still be relevant. I didn't see him in her future. Where are we going?" Zoey asked as she kept her pace with him.

"Emergency council meeting at Grand Mistress Lauren's."

Zoey ran next to Slade as they cut through a dark backyard and into Grand Mistress Lauren's backyard. The lights were on and her curtains were drawn. Slade knocked on the back door. When it opened, Neferu was there in a burnt gold tunic over leggings. It didn't matter that the tunic was modern, Neferu still looked like an Egyptian ruler from thousands of years ago.

"What is this emergency?" she asked in her superior tone that Zoey had learned wasn't her being unkind. It was just her. Neferu's long black hair laid stick straight down her back, but it was highlighted with streaks of steel gray, unsurprising considering she'd been around since before Cleopatra. Neferu and Cleopatra had been *besties*.

"I'll tell you once everyone is here," Slade told her, not intimidated at all. Zoey was still intimidated.

They stepped inside as Polly, Vilma, and Agnes *poofed* into the living room from their homes. Grand Master Linus was already there talking to Grand Mistress Lauren. Linus, Slade, Samuel, Niles, and Raiden made up the Tenebris council.

Zoey looked around and found Niles talking to Neferu. Neferu was the history keeper for the Claritase. Niles, while young in comparison to Neferu, was the history keeper for the Tenebris. Niles looked to be in his mid to late twenties, and Slade said he was a baby compared to Neferu's thousands of years, Niles was only about four hundred and twenty years old. However, he was a natural researcher who loved details and that made him perfect to be history keeper.

Raiden Ilmarinen was new to town. He looked to be a thirty year old elite soccer athlete, but was really almost eight hundred. He was the go-to guy on family trees and the newest appointee to the Tenebris council. Apparently family tree research was all there was to do in the cold Artic days and nights in Finland. Well, among other, hotter things. And hot he was. He had all the women, human and witches alike, swooning over his Nordic good looks.

At last, Samuel *poofed* into the room and Grand Mistress Lauren called the council to order and turned the meeting over to Slade. Zoey sat and listened as Slade and Samuel told of the night's events. What caught Zoey's eye was that neither Agnes nor Vilma didn't look as surprised as everyone else.

"Ian?" Lauren gasped in anger. Her teal eyes narrowed in anger. "I will root him out and hang him by his testicles from the tallest tree."

"Agnes? Vilma? Do you have something to add?" Zoey asked as she cocked her head at them.

"We had a feeling it was him," Agnes admitted. "The Irises and the Opossums have been reporting aliens in the woods." The Irises were a married women's club. The Opossums were a married men's club. You had to be married over twenty-five years to join either club. However, most of the members had been married closer to forty years. Agnes and Vilma were honorary Irises. They'd told the members that their husbands had passed away long ago. Which was true. They'd married humans and outlived them . . . and their children.

"Aliens? They think we're aliens?" Neferu spat.

"They saw red glowing lights coming from the woods," Agnes explained. Ian drew his power from the fire element.

"What are we going to do?" Polly asked, drawing attention back to the problem at hand.

"We need to figure out why he wants Jane and what these nightmares are that she's suffering through each night."

Lauren crossed her arms over her chest. "I don't like this. I feel as if Jane has lied to us."

"She was engaged to Ian before the wars. Does that help?" Zoey felt like she betrayed Jane's trust by telling the council, but it was clear all cards needed to be on the table.

"*Engaged!*" Lauren and Neferu skipped right past mad and went directly to enraged.

Linus held up a calming hand. "Raiden, can you look into the family trees to see if you can find a marriage contract? If a marriage was to be performed before the wars, there were contracts, just like the humans had."

Neferu stood and turned to the man who looked to be her opposite. Everywhere Neferu was dark, Raiden was light. "I'll summon Fern Langley. She's the family history expert for the Claritase. She's in the process of packing up to move here from New York City where she worked with the museum's ancient texts."

"We can send some men to move her," Master Linus said. "Niles, can you make that happen?"

"Yes, sir." In a flash, Niles was gone and so was Neferu. Zoey checked her watch, poor Fern was about to have a rude awakening.

"I think we need to move Jane," Zoey told the group. "If Ian is after her, we need to get her someplace safe."

Polly nodded her head in agreement, but Lauren shook hers.

"I want to get to the bottom of this first. We'll keep her safe until then."

"Dr. Sinclair will protect her," Slade told them.

"He's a human. He can be spelled," Samuel said cautiously. He didn't want to insult his best friend.

Slade shook his head. "Yes, he's human. Or at least I think he is. But he can't be spelled. I tried to get into his mind and couldn't. I tried to cast magic against him and couldn't."

"That's not possible," Raiden said, sounding shocked. Not with disrespect, but because it shouldn't be.

Suddenly, Neferu was back with a woman who looked as earthy as her name. Fern Langley looked to be a sweetheart. Her light brown hair was tucked behind her ears, but was wild everywhere else. It was clear she had come straight from bed. Her green eyes were focused though and the kind smile she wore as she pushed up her glasses made Zoey like her instantly.

"Grand Mistress Lauren," Fern said with a deep bow. "It's such an honor to meet you in person. I am truly touched that you approved my application to be head of genealogy for the Claritase. I haven't been around many of our kind in four hundred years," she said with tears in her eyes.

Raiden stepped forward and with an elegant bow handed her a tissue.

"Raiden Ilmarinen, at your service."

"Did you just sigh?" Slade whispered in Zoey's ear. Oops. What that out loud?

"Maybe," Zoey confessed.

"He may be older than me, but I have youth on my side. I'll show you the difference when we get home."

Zoey smothered a laugh. "It's all the same once you're older than five hundred, isn't it?"

Slade growled in return and it had Zoey biting back a smile. They needed to wrap this meeting up because she needed to kiss her true love something fierce.

"Raiden, I need you to take Fern to our records and fill her in on what's going on. Find out who Ian was engaged to and if there's any record of what happened. Did they marry?"

Fern gasped. "Ian? Married? If he were married, he'd have a claim to whoever his wife is. There's no time to lose."

Fern grabbed Raiden's hand and Zoey couldn't help but smile. Fern didn't make it to Raiden's chin, and the timid looking girl next door was suddenly looking rather fierce.

"Hang on." He told her as he wrapped his arm around her shoulder and then they *poofed* off to the hidden records.

"Neferu, I want you and Niles to work on finding out why Dr. Sinclair is immune to magic. I'll send word to Niles to wrap up the handling of Fern's apartment and meet you in the archives." Grand Mistress Lauren sent a text. Zoey almost laughed. All the magic in the world and texting was still the way to go.

"Thank you, Master Slade, for bringing this to our attention. Lauren and I will meet the prisoners tonight and wipe their memories after seeing them for ourselves," Linus said as he reached out to shake Slade's hand. "Keep the council informed."

"Come on, let's leave before she asks about my wedding dress," Zoey said with a wink to Grand Mistress Lauren as she grabbed her love's hand and *poofed* away.

9

"It was aliens."

"Peach, there is no such things as aliens in Moonshine Hollow." Otis, her husband of forty or so years groaned at his wife's declaration. "They're all out in Area-51. That's way on the other side of the country."

"Then you explain the crazy lights we all saw last night in the woods. They were so bright they woke Fay up," Peach said as she placed her hands on her hips.

"Fay likes to get in the moonshine," Billy Ray, the large lumberjack of a senior citizen who was the bartender at the married men's club, said. Zoey knew it to be the truth, Fay liked her drink. Only this time, Peach was right. There were lights and they did wake Fay up.

Sally June nodded her head and backed up her fellow Iris member. "Fay wasn't the only one who saw it. I saw it too. Are you going to say I was drunk on moonshine, Billy Ray?"

"Are you all talkin' about those lights?" Dale asked as he came into Zoey's shop. It wasn't even eight in the morning and the place was packed. Everyone was talking about the lights in the woods the night before. "Scared the hell out of my sheep."

"See? Young Dale saw them too," Peach said with validation.

"Yup. Woke up Maribelle and we stepped outside to watch them. Think they're the northern lights?" Dale asked.

"But these were red," Sally June pointed out.

Dale shrugged his wide shoulders and ran a hand over his neatly trimmed beard. He wore the perpetual smile of a newlywed, even when talking about mystery lights. "Yeah, but we're in the south. Maybe they're red down here?"

Zoey's morning went like this until she sold out of breakfast and shooed everyone from the shop. She needed to talk to Jane because this wasn't *southern lights*. It was Ian spelling people to kidnap Jane.

~

AIR. She needed air.

Jane opened her mouth on a gasp as her eyes flew open. The first thing she noticed was she was covered in sweat. The second was the man in her room. Before she knew it, her hands were raised and she drew all her magic to rush forward.

"Jane?"

Jane snapped her fingers closed, holding the magical energy in check. She felt it swirling down her arms and balling in the palms of her hand ready for release.

"Jane. It's me, Dr. Sinclair. It's okay. You just woke up from a night terror. I'm going to turn on the light, okay?"

Jane was breathing hard, trying to fill her body with as much oxygen as she could as she nodded her head at the shadow. She kept her arms outstretched and at the ready though.

Click.

The light reached every shadow in the room. Jane had to blink a few times, but then quickly lowered her arms when she saw Galen standing there.

"Here, let me get you untangled."

Jane looked down and saw the cords from the sleep study equipment tangled about her. She sat still as Galen slowly moved toward her. She hated the look in his eyes. There was pity in that look and she was never one to want pity. There was no question now. She'd find out what she was dreaming about and then she'd disappear. She could reinvent herself in a blink of an eye . . . or the wiggle of a finger.

"What did you find out?" Jane asked as she tried to ignore the brush of Galen's fingers over her skin as he removed the equipment.

"The reason you're so tired is that you never get restful sleep. It takes you much longer to fall into REM sleep than it should. Then when you do, you're gripped with night terrors. I'm going to write up the report, and then I'd like to discuss it with you. I think it might help you figure out what you're dreaming about."

Jane took a deep breath and shoved her hair from her face. "Okay. When do you want to meet?"

"Tomorrow is the soonest I can finish it. I can call you when I get it completed."

Jane nodded. The feeling to run was almost completely overwhelming.

"There's one more thing."

"What?" Jane asked. She could hear the foreboding in his voice. Whatever it was, it wasn't good.

"Jud broke into your house last night and tried to kidnap you."

Jane blinked. She processed the words, but they didn't make sense. "Jud from town?"

"Yes. It was bizarre. But he said he had to get you."

"Me? What would he want with—?" Jane snapped her mouth shut as a shiver ran down her spine. Could it be Ian? "What happened to him?"

"I knocked him out and then the sheriff and his deputy took him to jail."

Thank goodness the sheriff and the deputy were witches. Surely they read Jud's mind and could tell her what was going on. They probably made sure Galen had his story straight too. But just in case . . .

Jane focused her magic on Galen's brain. She'd just make sure Slade wiped all that he needed to. Only when she tried to enter his thoughts she was met with a brick wall. No matter how she tried to get in, she couldn't.

Jane might not use her powers much, but she had them. Lots of them. It was why Ian was after her. But no matter what she did, she couldn't get into Galen's mind. That didn't make sense. He was human.

The doorbell rang and Galen spun as if to put himself between her and whoever might come in. Darned if that didn't make her heart beat faster even though it was more likely she'd need to protect him.

"I'll just see who that is while you get dressed."

"Thank you, Dr. Sinclair."

He looked back at her and smiled. "Anything for you."

Then her heart did more than beat faster. It fell completely in love with Galen Sinclair. And then it broke when she realized she was going to have to leave him behind when she ran from Ian. If Ian had sent Jud after her, everyone in Moonshine Hollow was in danger.

JANE QUICKLY DRESSED and rushed from her bedroom when she heard the front door close. Galen was gone, but her house wasn't empty. Zoey sat on the couch waiting for her.

"What you are doing here?" Jane asked, but then realized how rude that sounded. "Shouldn't you be at your store?"

"Sold out within two hours. Come sit down. I'll get coffee and breakfast."

As Jane sat down, Zoey wiggled her fingers and two cups of coffee and two extra large double chocolate cupcakes appeared before her.

"I must admit it, I miss my magic," Jane said.

"So, use it," Zoey encouraged with a shrug.

Jane took a deep breath. Was it really that easy? "I've been hiding for so long and using magic can draw a hunter's attention."

"But you're not alone now and most of the hunters are dead or captured."

"Except one."

Zoey set her cupcake down. "We need to talk about Ian."

"You read me. You know I was engaged to him. That's it."

"Jane," Zoey said, reaching out and taking Jane's hand in hers. Jane was forced to turn and look at her then. "I'm not reading you. I won't do that without your permission. I know that's not it. I also know you're not in league with him in anyway. But I also know you haven't been honest with me about your past."

"What do you mean?" Jane tried to keep her cool, but

even as she spoke calmly, she was gathering her power to *poof* away as soon as Zoey let go of her hand.

"I mean the fact that Ian is using magic to send humans to kidnap you. I mean the fact that no one on the council knows a Jane Farrow. I mean the fact that you might as well tell us since Raiden Ilmarinen and Fern Langley, the top Tenebris and Claritase genealogists, are researching who you really are. You know it won't take Fern and Raiden long to find the truth. Jane, let me help you. You ran here for safety. Now let me keep you safe." Zoey didn't drop her hand and then she frowned. "You're going to run, aren't you?"

"You said you wouldn't read me!" Jane shouted as she tried to pull her hand from Zoey's.

Suddenly warmth spread in her hand and coursed up her arm until Jane's whole body was cocooned in warmth. Then Zoey dropped her hand. Jane tried to transport, but she couldn't. "What did you do?"

"I'm keeping you safe, even if it means from yourself. Call me when you're ready to talk."

"What is this?" Jane yelled as she tried to leave her house, but wasn't able to get past the door to follow Zoey outside.

"I'm grounding you, Jane." Zoey turned around and Jane's anger fell when she saw the tears in Zoey's eyes. "Do you think I want to do this? I felt your magic. *It* reached out and touched me. It told me you were going to run, and while your mind thinks it's the best thing to do, your magic told me otherwise. It's crying out for help, Jane. Let me help you."

"I can't put you in danger!" Jane shouted back.

"Keeping me in the dark is putting me at greater risk than confiding in me. Jane, your nightmares are getting worse. You were yelling Ian's name last night in your sleep.

While you're directly affected by it, you have to see that Ian is a threat to not just you, but to all of us."

Jane crossed her arms over her chest. Zoey was right, but she couldn't get the words to come out.

"I'll stop by tomorrow to see if you've changed your mind. If you need Slade or me for any reason, all you have to do is think our names and we'll know it and be there. I'm sorry, Jane. I wish it were different."

Jane watched Zoey walk down the street. Jane was so angry, she could barely see straight. She was angry at Zoey. She was angry at Ian. She was angry at the council. She was angry at herself. Jane slammed the front door and dropped down onto her couch. On the table, there were now over a dozen cupcakes and even lunch and dinner. Zoey was looking out for her even when Jane didn't let herself trust anyone.

Jane took a deep breath and turned her attention inward. Her mind and magic were at war inside of her. Her mind told her to run. Her magic told her to stand her ground. The question was which should she listen to.

10

GALEN TOOK a long nap before he began working on Jane's report. It would take time going through all the audio and visual materials. He turned them on to play, knowing she wouldn't be talking for most of the eight hours she slept. As they played silently in the background, Galen began to go over the data he had collected.

Hours later, Galen was done with his data report and was about to heat up some leftovers when the tapes played the moment Jane shot straight up in bed and screamed, "Ian!"

For the next four hours, Galen sat in silence and watched the torment of whatever it was that went on in Jane's mind. His heart broke for her but his determination to get to the bottom of her night terrors only increased.

It was close to midnight when he was done with the report. Galen wanted to call Jane, but instead closed his laptop and went to bed. He'd see her in the morning and do everything in his power to get these terrors to stop.

As he fell asleep, his mind and heart were on Jane. He didn't have a word for it because it seemed so irrational, but it was as if fate were pulling them together. *Never deter the hand of fate, boy. She's even more fickle than a Selkie.*

Galen fell asleep with a smile on his face at the memory of his Nan. Well, if fate wanted them together, who was he to say no?

JANE CROSSED her arms over her chest and stared with anger at her quickly filling living room. There had been no knocking. They'd just shown up. It wasn't even eight in the morning when the first person arrived in her living room.

Fortunately, Grand Mistress Lauren was the one behind the gathering, because after spending yesterday "grounded," Jane was ready to let Zoey have it.

Knock, knock.

Jane spun around and opened the door to find Zoey, Slade, and Magnus standing there. "Thank you for knocking. The rest of the council didn't bother with it."

Zoey rolled her eyes. "Ugh. I know! It's so rude."

Jane opened the door wide as Slade and his father-in-law to be walked into to join the rest of those already gathered. Zoey reached out and clasped Jane's hand. "I'm so sorry. I hate being heavy-handed, but I couldn't let you leave. Everything depends on—" Zoey's eyes went blank. Her hand tightened and a tear rolled down her cheek.

"Zoey?" Slade shoved past Jane and wrapped his arms around his true love. Zoey didn't move. It was if she were in a trance—a trance that started when she touched Jane.

"Should I yank my hand away?" Jane whispered as suddenly she felt the entire council behind her.

"No!" Grand Mistress Lauren called out. "She's having a vision. Let it happen."

The distress on Zoey's face told Jane everything she needed to know about this vision. It was horrible, and it had to do with her. It felt like an eternity but finally Zoey dropped her hand and blinked her eyes. Tears rolled down both cheeks now as terror replaced the blank stare of her eyes.

Slade lifted her into his arms and hurried her inside. Jane shut the door as he took a seat with Zoey on his lap. Her face was buried his neck as she wept openly. Jane looked around and saw the concern on the council's faces. Jane had told herself they were uncaring but that wasn't true at all. They were the complete opposite. The pain in Grand Mistress Lauren's face and Grand Master Linus's stance told her that they cared deeply for Zoey and what she was feeling. Polly had tears in her own eyes. Even Neferu, the coldest witch Jane had ever met, looked upset.

"I'm so sorry," Zoey finally said. "Jane, you *have* to stay in Moonshine Hollow. If not, Moonshine will be burned to the ground when it's discovered you're not here. There was so much screaming. So much death. Oh Goddess, the screams."

"Why me?" Jane managed to finally say.

"I don't know. My vision showed me first what would happen if you left. The screaming, the ash, the death of every human here . . . then it showed me something else. You were there, Jane. All of us were there together. And then the blood came. But because we were together we survived. We have to tackle whatever is coming *together*."

Jane looked around the room as she was struck by a sudden realization that had her taking a step back as if to steady herself. She wasn't alone. She wasn't the only witch who had been hiding and running for four hundred years. Everyone in the room had been too. "No more running."

Polly was the first to reach her and pull her into a hug. "No more running," she whispered to Jane. "We're all here for you."

"Do you want to tell them, or do you want us to?" A cute little woman with green eyes and light brown hair asked sympathetically.

"Are you Fern?" Jane asked her.

"Yes, it's nice to meet you." She held out her hand and the two earth witches shared a moment together as they shook. Their powers recognized each other and Fern smiled at Jane's shocked expression. "I'm your cousin on your mother's side."

"I didn't know I had family on my mom's side."

"Your father insisted on separating from everyone in his life. He sensed that you were valuable to the wrong type of people."

"Too bad he handed me over to the wrong type of person."

Fern nodded understandingly. "You're not alone anymore. You have family. My parents are still living and they'll be thrilled to meet you."

Jane didn't know what to say. She wasn't alone in this world after all. She had thought her mother's family was dead. She'd never met them and it had always just been her parents and her father's sister.

"I can tell everyone what we found," Fern whispered with a nod of her head to the Viking standing near her. That must be Raiden. "If it's too hard for you to do so."

Jane shook her head. "No. It's time for me to tell my story. You're right," Jane said a little louder now as she looked around the room. "I'm not alone anymore."

GALEN PACKED up his things and looked at his watch. It was just after eight in the morning. He would stop by and pick up breakfast and then head over to Jane's. Maybe he'd catch her before work.

When Galen opened the door to Zoey's Sweet Treats, he was surprised to see the long line. There was usually a line but normally it *moved*. This one seemed to be going slow as molasses.

"What's going on?" Galen asked Peach, who was standing in front of him in line. She'd been happy to make an appointment with Galen, but her husband had refused and wanted to see Dr. Thurman.

"Zoey had a meeting she couldn't miss, so Maribelle and Dale are filling in for her. But bless their hearts, they're mixing up orders left and right. I'd take a seat if I were you, this is going to take a bit."

Galen smiled kindly and pulled out one of the nearby bistro chairs for Peach. Peach made sure to point out his manners to her husband who just rolled his eyes as he talked to other members of the Opossums.

"So, did you see the aliens the other night?" Peach asked as soon as Galen took the chair opposite her.

"Aliens?" Galen asked with surprise. That wasn't what he was expecting from Peach. Gossip, sure. But aliens?

Peach leaned in closer and dropped her voice. "I think the sheriff is in on it."

"You think Sheriff Slade is an alien?" Galen asked slowly as he reevaluated the physical he'd given Peach. Maybe he should send her for a CT head scan.

Peach nodded and looked around to make sure no one was listening. "He told me there's no such things as aliens, but then told us not to go into the woods for the next week while he investigates."

The bell over the door tinkled and Galen looked up to see Jud walking in the door. Galen acted on instinct and before he knew it, he had handfuls of Jud's shirt in his fists as he shoved him out the door he just walked into. Galen heard everyone stop talking and knew they were watching, but he didn't care. This man had tried to hurt Jane. Why was he just waltzing about?

"Doc?" Jud gasped in surprise as Galen shoved him against the door to keep it closed so the people inside couldn't come out and break them up. "Thanks for fixin' up my broken nose. I promise I'll pay you."

"Pay me? You tried to hurt someone I care about," Galen growled.

"Hurt someone? I wouldn't hurt anyone." Jud looked so surprised that Galen had to stop and think. No, there was the broken nose he had given him. But he didn't reset it, so who did?

"You tried to hurt Jane."

"Jane who?" Jud asked.

"Jane Farrow."

"The nice lady at the forest station? Why would I want to hurt her?"

Galen believed the complete innocence in his eyes. But still . . . "Two nights ago, where were you?"

"I went huntin' for the weekend with some friends. It was dark out and then there was this light. I tripped and smashed my face into a tree. My buddies brought me to you and you put my nose back into place. Then I went home. Why?"

Galen dropped his hands and took a step back. What the heck was going on? He looked into the bakery and saw Peach's face pressed against the glass. "Aliens," she mouthed. Maybe she was right.

Selkie.

His Nan's voice was clear as day and he snapped his head to see if she were standing next to him. Instead, there were just curious stares of people waiting to get into the bakery.

"Sorry. I'm glad your nose is feeling better. Excuse me."

He needed to see Jane. He needed to find out what the heck was happening.

11

JANE TOOK A DEEP BREATH. Her hands were clasped tightly as she stood in front of a living room full of powerful witches. Jane was petrified that as soon as she revealed her secrets they would turn against her. She was supposed to have been Ian's wife—Ian, one of the most hated Tenebris witches there ever was. However, it was time to place her trust in someone, and while she didn't necessarily trust everyone on the council, she did trust Zoey.

"I was to marry Ian on the night of the great treachery. I was his intended." Jane tried to say it loudly and clearly, but her voice broke. No one said a word. They all stared at her and Jane thought about bolting, but knew she couldn't run again. No more running.

"I didn't know about the treason. I lost both my parents and my aunt that night." Jane took a deep breath as her mind left the safety of the living room and transported back to that horrible night. "'Go to Ian. He will keep you safe,' my father ordered before dying. Little did I know at that time that it was Ian who'd killed him. My father's sister grabbed me and took me to Ian's rooms after we grabbed some supplies to flee with. I found out then that Ian didn't want to marry me because he loved he. He didn't even care if I lived. He had to marry me first and then I could choose . . . die or join him and rule over the Claritase as he ruled over the Tenebris."

The room was quiet. Jane took a deep breath to continue, but Slade interrupted her. "Alexander was to rule. Why would Ian think he could?"

"The marriage contract my father signed with Ian gave him enough of my powers that he'd be stronger than Alexander," Jane finally admitted, and she was ready for the next question when it came.

"Who are you?" Grand Mistress Lauren asked. That was the million dollar question, wasn't it? In her body ran the power of ancient witches from both her father's and her mother's side of the family.

Jane took a wider stance as if to brace herself. "I am the only child of Emmerich and Deci Farrington."

Vilma snorted. Agnes rolled her eyes. Lauren and Linus shared a look. Neferu shook her head.

"What?" Jane demanded.

"Your father was a prick," Vilma said bluntly.

Jane opened her mouth, but Agnes stopped her. "Don't get us wrong. We never heard of him abusing your mother, but he was paranoid. He thought he was so superior to everyone else because of his family line, so being around we mere originals was beneath him."

Neferu nodded. "I knew your mother before they married and she was the nicest woman. I see that in you. I see her in you. But they're right, your father was a narcissistic ass. It doesn't surprise me one bit that he agreed to give some of your powers to Ian to build a dynasty."

Jane stood in shock. She didn't know what to say. She didn't know what to feel. She'd been mad at her father for his isolating and demanding ways, but she still loved him.

Grand Mistress Lauren reached out and touched her hand. "I understand this hurts. It's never easy for a daughter to hear that her father wasn't perfect."

"I was so mad that he arranged my marriage. I never understood why, but I did love him," Jane admitted.

"Of course you did, dear," Vilma said, joining Jane and giving her a hug. "Now everything makes sense. Dear, you have family. The Langleys are your mother's people. And through some marriages, you're part of my family."

"And mine," Agnes told her, joining them too and pulling her into another hug.

"Your ancient lines make you family to most of us originals," Linus explained.

"Not mine."

Jane laughed even as tears started. "Thanks, Neferu."

The ancient witch shrugged, but Jane saw the small twitch of her lips.

"I'm really not alone, am I?" Jane asked.

"No, and my whole family will be here soon to welcome you." Fern pushed aside the older witches and flung herself into Jane's arms.

"This all makes sense now," Slade said as he clenched his jaws. "He thinks the marriage contract is still binding."

"I don't understand," Zoey said, and as such a new witch, she wouldn't.

"Back in the middle ages contract marriages were all the rage," Neferu began to explain. "The humans were doing it and we thought we should too. It was a way to ensure powerful lines. Heads of the most powerful families made contracts between their children. Sometimes money was exchanged as a dowry for the bride, sometimes land, and sometimes powers. That was the worst. It was cruel and diminished the role of Claritase everywhere. For instance, Jane's mother was way more powerful than her husband and I think he resented it. That's why I'm not surprised he used Jane's powers as a dowry."

"Surely a contract over four hundred years old isn't valid anymore." Jane could see Zoey's mind running through all the possibilities.

"This isn't the human legal system," Niles told Zoey. "Our lives are long and so are our contracts."

"For how long?" Zoey asked.

"Five hundred years," Niles explained. "It's no wonder Jane has been running. Ian can still enforce the contract. The only way he can't is if he can't find her for the next century or so."

"We must protect you," Linus said with urgency.

"I don't know what to do. I was going to run and do that, but Zoey's vision—" Jane was so confused. Her life had been so simple up until now. Hide from Ian. That was it. Now there was a vision and one didn't ignore an actual vision sent from the Goddess of creation herself.

"Samuel is a strong warrior. He can move in with you until Ian is captured."

Jane heard someone suck in air and suddenly saw Polly standing ramrod straight as she bit her lower lip.

"No," Zoey said firmly.

Agnes narrowed her eyes and stared at Jane. "You have another secret."

"No, I don't. I've told you everything about my past."

"Your past, but not your present," Agnes said cryptically.

"I don't understand," Jane said slowly. She'd been truthful with everyone.

The knock on the door had a roomful of witches whipping their hands up and enough electricity from the powers surging forward to make Jane's hair float up a little.

"It's okay," Jane told them. "It's Galen . . . I mean Dr. Sinclair."

"And there it is," Agnes said with a smile as she lowered her hands.

"What is?" Jane really felt as if she were missing something.

"How did you know it was Dr. Sinclair?" Grand Mistress Lauren asked curiously as there was another knock on the door. "Tell him to hold on."

"I'll be right there!" Jane called out and the knocking stopped. "How did I know it was him?" She had no idea. She just knew. "I don't know. I just knew it was him. Why?" Everyone looked at each other with disbelief and Jane once again felt as if she were missing something. "Spit it out!" she snapped.

Slade shifted on his feet and suddenly looked uncomfortable when everyone turned to look at him and Zoey to explain. "Um, you see, when a man and a woman—"

Jane rolled her eyes. "I didn't have sex with him."

"You don't need to have sex to fall in love," Slade said, looking considerably more awkward as he cleared his throat.

Jane's mouth dropped open. Love? Who said anything about love?

"Well now, this is *very* interesting," Mistress Lauren said with a surprised look. "Get the door, dear."

GALEN WAS WIRED. His whole body seemed to be on edge as

he banged on Jane's door. It was a feeling unlike anything he'd experienced before. He *needed* to get to her right now. He needed to see with his own eyes that she was safe. The door opened and Jane was finally there.

"What's happened?" Galen asked as he saw the look on her face. She looked overwhelmed and bewildered with a hint of stubbornness on her face.

"Nothing. What's up?"

Galen narrowed his eyes at the way she only cracked the door an inch and used her body to block his ability to see inside. Something was making her upset. He knew it. "Just let the guy in," Galen heard a male voice say from somewhere in the living room.

Galen placed his hand on the door above Jane's head and pushed it open. She stepped back, looking guilty. She shouldn't look or even feel guilty. They weren't dating. Even if he'd already planned to discharge her as his patient and assign a friend from Knoxville to be her new doctor. Even if he'd already planned on coming over her to ask her to go out on a real date. And even if his heart had already filled with love for her, it didn't mean they were actually together.

Galen took a calming breath as he looked around room in surprise. It wasn't a guy. Well, it was numerous men *and* women. "I'm sorry. I didn't know you had company. Hi, Sheriff, Zoey, Lauren. I'm sorry. I'm new and I don't know the rest of you. I'm Galen Sinclair."

Galen smiled and then winced. The embarrassment of storming into Jane's house was giving him a stress headache. He put his fingers to the middle of his forehead and pressed. The pain stopped as everyone in the room stared at him.

"Is something the matter? You all look worried." Galen took a step closer to Jane to be there if she needed support.

"We were just talking about the importance of family," replied Lauren, who worked in the clinic with him. "Galen is the new doctor in town. I don't think you and I have ever talked about your family while at work."

Galen shrugged. "My parents are professors in the Northeast. I was super close to my Nan, but she passed away two years ago."

"I'm so sorry." Jane reached out to him and when she placed her hand on his arm he felt completely at peace.

"Dr. Sinclair, who are your people?" Neferu demanded.

Galen saw Jane and Zoey roll their eyes and relaxed a little. This wasn't a hostile takeover, just a woman who gets right to the point. He didn't think his family was that interesting.

"My people?" Galen asked, not fully understanding. Didn't he just tell them about his family?

"Where do they come from?" Neferu clarified.

"Oh, Scotland," Galen told them. "Family lore says we were once a powerful family in Northern Scotland. My Nan was the last of our branch of the family still on the island of Orkney. Don't worry. No one knows where it is. It's about five miles north of the mainland of Scotland."

"The Standing Stones of Stenness are there," Linus told the room. Galen nodded and noticed the other people in the room were whispering to each other.

"I'm being so rude," Lauren said with a laugh. "Let me introduce you to our little gathering. You know Zoey, Slade, and Samuel. Magnus here is Zoey's father. And have you met Agnes and Vilma?"

Galen smiled at the elderly women. "Oh, yes. They brought me a welcome basket of the local moonshine."

"Excellent. Then this is my dear friend, Linus," Lauren

introduced as Galen shook his hand. The man had a long beard and looked like he belonged on the steps of the Parthenon back in ancient Greece. "And this is Neferu, Polly, Fern, Niles, and Raiden."

"I'm from England," Fern said as she shook his hand. "I've visited the standing stones on Orkney a very long time ago. There was a woman on the island who was the caretaker of the stones. I believe her last name was Sinclair."

Galen was shocked and instantly smiled. "Yes! That was Nan. When were you there?"

"Oh, ninety—" Fern stopped suddenly and giggled. "Sometime in the late nineties. I can't remember exactly when. I was just a kid."

"We have to go," Neferu said suddenly as she grabbed Niles by the hand. "We have work to do." Wow, that was some cougar action right there. Niles looked to be in his mid to late twenties while Neferu appeared to be in her fifties. Well, to each their own.

"It was nice meeting you." Galen called out as the couple headed out the front door.

"What brought you by this morning?" Zoey asked.

"I wanted to go over Jane's sleep test results. I can come back since you all are . . . busy?" His statement turned into more of a question as he looked for an idea of what they were up to.

"Wedding planning," Zoey's father said with a chuckle as he slapped Galen on the back. Ugh. Now Galen's headache was like a jackhammer. But as suddenly as it came on, it left again. "Why don't you take Jane into her bedroom to discuss the results in private. We can wait."

"Thank you," Galen said slowly, feeling as if maybe he should leave them, but everything in him had him reaching for Jane and telling him to hold on to her and never let her go.

"Right this way," Jane said, and Galen's whole body reacted when he heard that slight breathlessness in her voice. Maybe he wasn't the only one who felt such a strong reaction between them.

12

"WHAT THE HELL IS GOING ON?" Zoey whispered as everyone came to stand close together. "I can't read him at all. Like, *none* of my magic worked."

Her father shook his head. "Neither did mine."

"Or mine," Lauren confirmed.

"I got nothing," Linus told them as everyone else agreed.

"Why isn't our magic working on him?" Zoey asked.

"I have a theory, but Neferu and Niles can tell us for sure when they get back," Fern whispered.

"We still have the issue of Jane needing protection," Lauren reminded them. "Ian is still out there."

"I'll gather a group to guard the woods." Zoey didn't want to think of her love up against Ian, but if anyone could take him on, it was Slade.

"I'll help," Samuel offered to Slade.

"I'll help too." Raiden stepped across the circle to join Slade and Samuel.

"We will stay with Jane," Agnes said as she volunteered herself and Vilma for guard duty.

"As soon as Neferu and Niles have something, we will

regroup and decide how best to protect Jane and capture Ian. This threat must end," Lauren hissed angrily.

JANE SAT on her bed and watched as Galen tried to decide where to sit. It was almost funny as she could tell he wanted to be next to her, but wanted to stay professional at the same time.

In the end he set his bag on the dresser and pulled out the papers he had inside before leaning back against it. He began with filling her in on her vitals. Jane sat quietly as she didn't want to burst his bubble by telling him she knew her vitals were perfect. It was one of the perks of being a healing witch.

"I think your night terrors were triggered by a trauma. I've written down everything you said during your sleep. Can you tell me about it?"

Shoot. What had she said? Jane tried to be casual when she took the paper. Ian. His name was all over it. So was the mention of her arms out stretched as if she were using her powers. What was Ian doing to her in her dreams?

"Jane, who is Ian?" Galen asked quietly.

Jane didn't know what to say. She looked down at what she'd screamed in her sleep. *I won't let you take them. I won't let you hurt me. I'll kill you.* In her nightmares, she was still strong. She needed to find that strength again. She did run from Ian. She'd beaten him back twice now.

She felt the magic spark in her fingers. In her dreams she'd defended herself with magic. It was time to remember how to use it. It was time to ask for help. It was time to trust again. "Someone my parents pushed me to marry. I didn't want to, so I ran away. I've been running ever since."

Galen was quiet, but Jane saw his knuckles turn white as

he clenched the dresser top he was leaning against. "He wants to hurt you?"

"Yes." Jane took a deep breath. It was as if a weight was lifted. She wasn't alone anymore. "And I'm done running. My friends are going to help me."

Galen stepped forward and then went down to his knees in front of her. "Let me help too."

"I'd like that. How about dinner tonight? I can cook this time."

"I'll be here by six."

Jane smiled at Galen and reached for him. She placed her hands on his shoulders and felt magic stir deep within her along with a rush of emotion. "Thank you, Galen."

Jane was about to let go when Galen leaned forward and closed his eyes. His lips brushed questioningly against hers and when she leaned into him he deepened the kiss. Sparks flew. Literally. One landed on the hem of her shirt and Jane smelled smoke.

She slapped her hand down on it and tried to pretend that hadn't happened.

"Wow," Galen said, opening his eyes from the kiss. He looked as dazed as Jane felt. "That was magical. I'm not one to wax poetic, but a single kiss has never felt so right before. Was it just me?"

"No, it wasn't just you. There is something, um, magical between us." In fact, they were so hot together they could start a fire.

᛫ Galen's eyes suddenly creased as he leaned forward. "Huh. I thought your eyes were green. They remind me of the fields in Scotland."

"They are green," Jane said with a little laugh.

"They have gold flecks in them. They're beautiful."

Her eyes didn't have gold flecks in them. As an earth

witch, her eyes were solid green representing her powers. "I don't have gold flecks," she laughed and then looked closer at his brown eyes. "But you do."

Galen laughed and shook his head. "No, I have brownish-amber eyes. But look at us trying to talk about each other's eyes so romantically and blowing it so badly. Jane," he said, brushing a strand of hair behind her ear, "I'm glad you feel it too."

"Jane!" Jane smiled as she heard Agnes call out.

"Be right there!"

Galen stood and held out his hand for her to take. Jane placed her hand in his and felt powerful. He liked her as much as she liked him and there was something special about that. She could feel their connection grow as they walked to the living room hand in hand.

"Oh my Goddess," Lauren gasped as she stared at them.

Galen chuckled. "I haven't heard that saying since my Nan. She said it was because women are the healers of the world."

Jane froze. Her heart beat so loud she knew all the witches in the room could hear it.

"Well, time to go. We need to get back to wedding planning," Vilma said as she grabbed Galen by the arm and practically shoved him out the door.

Everyone else stood silently in shock.

"He's not a witch, though, right?" Jane finally asked into the silence.

"I don't know what he is," Linus muttered as they all stared at the closed door.

"When he kissed me there was a spark," Jane confessed. She had decided to embrace her power and there was always power in the truth.

"That's nice, dear," Agnes said absently. "Sexual chemistry is important in a relationship."

Jane held up the hem of her shirt to show them where it was clearly burned through. "No, I mean there were literal sparks."

Again, everyone was quiet as they stared at her.

"We need to go help Neferu and Niles," Fern said, suddenly grabbing Raiden and *poof* they were gone.

"I agree completely. We'll meet back here as soon as we have anything. In the meantime, Vilma and Agnes are going to stay with you," Lauren told her. It wasn't a question. It was a command but before Jane could argue, they were gone.

"Zoey, wait."

Zoey smiled kindly at her and reached for her hand. "I'm not going anywhere."

"But we are. We'll start patrols," Slade told them with a nod to Samuel.

"Be safe!" Polly called out as they left. "Do you want me to leave too?"

Jane shook her head. "Actually, if you all could stay it would be great. I need help finding my powers. I've suppressed them for so long in order to hide, but in my nightmares I use them to fight Ian. I think my powers are trying to tell me to use them. I'm hoping my terrors will stop once I feel confident in my powers again."

"Perfect," Zoey said, holding out her other hand to her father. "We can have a group lesson!"

"Then let's get to work," Polly told them as Agnes and Vilma rolled up their sleeves.

"We're going to zap that little bugger," Vilma said before sending a zap of magic right at Jane.

Jane's hands flashed up and a spark shot out of her

fingertips and then sputtered. "Ow!" Jane shook her hands at the sting of Vilma's magic. "What was that for?"

"To wake you up. Let's get started," Vilma said as she aimed her fingers and shot.

13

JANE WAS EXHAUSTED BUT EXHILARATED. Her powers were finally free and it was as if her magic was singing with joy. It had taken all morning and afternoon, but she could call them forth whenever she wanted to now. She was remembering old lessons and learning new ones.

Zoey and her father had helped Jane more than Polly, Agnes, and Vilma. It was clear that the Rode family had powers that were stronger than the Farrington family, and Jane bet stronger than the grand master and grand mistress, too.

"Was I too hard on you?" Magnus asked as everyone sat down for a restorative drink Agnes made.

Jane smiled at the man who looked like a thirty something but who acted liked a strange combination of warrior, teacher, and father. "No. You taught me so much. I feel so . . . energized. I also feel much more secure in my abilities."

Suddenly there was a person next to her on the couch and Jane fell to the side and let her magic fly.

Neferu flicked the hit away and looked annoyed. "Well, I

see it's been a productive day all around. Did you find your powers hidden away in a tomb?"

Jane cocked her head and looked over the elegant and subtly powerful woman. "I can't tell if you actually care or if you're just a bit— "

"Okay!" Zoey said, leaping into the conversation. "Jane did a lot of training today. What about you?"

Jane saw Neferu's lips twitch, and she didn't know if it was a smile or a curse.

"Niles, Fern, Raiden, and I did a lot of work," Neferu said, running a hand down her black slacks.

Jane noticed the others were standing by the kitchen table talking to Lauren and Linus. The whole crew was almost here in a blink. A second later, Zoey answered the door before there was a knock as Slade and Samuel walked in.

"What's going on?" Jane asked.

"We have news," Neferu said as she stood up.

"Tell us what you've found," Lauren said as they walked into the living room.

Jane didn't know if she wanted to hear it. The way Galen mentioned his Nan had her wondering if he was part witch, and she didn't know what to make of any of it. Something she hadn't told the group was that the Stones of Stenness held a place in her family history. She had planned on telling them that night.

"Galen Sinclair is not a witch," Neferu told them and Jane didn't know whether to be happy or sad about that. If he were human, it meant he'd live a normal human life, which was a blink of the eye in terms of her life expectancy.

"The Standing Stones of Stenness are very important to witches the world over," Fern said, taking over for Neferu. Jane was surprised, but she tried not to show it. She thought the stones were only important to her family, not all witches.

"For thousands of years, witches have consulted the stone keeper for advice. Witches have joined in meditation to speak to the Goddess at these stones and have sought the stones' healing powers to help restore their magic," Fern continued.

"Wait," Jane stopped her. "I knew that about the stones from my family. My father consulted the stone keeper on my marriage, but we never encountered any other witches there. Were there other stones that also held this power, like Stonehenge? I'm afraid my isolation has hindered my learning."

Fern shook her head. "Stonehenge is a human creation that we happily welcome as the main attraction of that kind for the British Isles. The truly magical stones are spread around the world. North Carolina, Scotland, England, Ireland, Bulgaria, Morocco, Japan, Poland . . . we have them all over. We did not set the stones in place or create the circles. We don't know who made them, but powerful magic is within them. If it was the Goddess, it would make sense, but sometimes standing stones are infused with dark magic. For all light, there is dark. It's the balance of life. We've done our best to bury those though. The stones in the small, and at the time, very isolated Orkney Islands are important right now because of what came with them. Or, I should say, who. Niles?"

Niles stood up as Fern sat down and cleared his throat. "The stone keeper. The first one appeared with the Stenness stones a little over five thousand years ago. They lived in a small cottage near the stones and were a guardian of sorts to both the stones and the witches who visited them."

Jane listened to the history of her people and found

herself feeling so angry with her parents. They had told her how special she was and that was why she lived in relative isolation from other witches because they'd be jealous of her and want her power. No one here was trying to take her power. They were trying to protect her and teach her; they weren't even making fun of her for not knowing what other witches appeared to already know.

"There have been two stone keepers over the past five thousand years or so. First the man. Then after he retired, his wife became the keeper of the stones."

"But"—Jane interrupted him as her mind processed it all, "that means the stone keeper I saw when my father sought advice on my marriage contract was Galen's Nan?"

"Yes, but let's not jump ahead. This is where things get interesting," Niles said. He turned to Raiden, "Tell them what we found."

"We were looking over the records of Mariam Sinclair, the last stone keeper, who died two years ago. We wanted to find out if Galen was really her grandson. It appears each stone keeper at Stenness lives approximately five thousand years. The husband died eight years ago, then Mariam two. The husband was six years older. That's all we really have to go on. We found out that, yes, Galen really is the grandson. Not only that, but his father is almost five thousand years old."

"Excuse me, what?" Jane blinked in surprise. "How old is Galen?"

"It appears Galen is thirty-six. It also appears his mother is sixty years old. His father's appearance is similar to what you'd see in a human in his mid-seventies. We found records of numerous marriages over the years, but it wasn't until he married his current wife that things changed. According to Mariam's journals, her son married his soul mate forty years ago and only then was he blessed with his first and only child, Galen. Four thousand plus years of marriages and not a single child. Mariam believed it was because true love plays a role in producing children for her family."

"So, Galen's father is the new stone keeper?" Zoey asked what Jane was wondering.

"Again, we found the answer in Mariam's journals. Her son knows about the keeping of the stones. He knows about witches and was raised to take over the job, but he was born when his parents were first married. He's approaching the end of his life in another twenty years. When Mariam asked him to take over, he declined. He wants to spend the last decades of his life with his wife. Mariam worried that meant the end to the stone keepers since Galen appears to be aging at a normal human rate."

"Do the other stones have stone keepers? Maybe they can cover two locations?" Jane suggested.

"There is another family of stone keepers who had thirteen children who are all keepers at different locations. However, the Stones of Stenness are the most powerful," Raiden explained. "We actually tried taking some of them to the stones and the stones wouldn't let them into the Sinclair cottage."

Raiden smiled then and Jane knew he wasn't done yet. "So—"

"So, we kept reading Mariam's journals and found her last entry. That morning she'd gone to the stones to commune with the Goddess. She had a vision she'd seen before. A vision of a couple, but now after almost four hundred plus years she knew who they were. She saw them leading the next generation of young witches into the future. She wrote that while she saw the vision, she heard words spoken to her and she raced home to write them down. It was a letter to Galen conferring unto him and his true love all powers of the stone keeper jointly for the next five thousand years and then unto their children who find their true love matches for the rest of time."

"Oh my Goddess," Zoey said slowly as everyone nodded and stared at Jane with wonder. "You're the stone keeper."

"What? No I'm not. Galen and I just met and he doesn't even know about witches. Plus it's his grandmother who bound me to Ian."

"What did your father tell you about that night?" Neferu demanded.

"That the stone keeper agreed with the match. My mother and I were against it, but my father went into the cottage and spoke with the stone keeper. I remember standing there with my mother in the stones as we opened our magic to them asking for guidance. The door to the cottage opened. My father bowed to the stone keeper and she nodded to my mother and me. Then the door closed and my father told us she'd agreed with him. The contract was signed and I've been haunted by it ever since."

Neferu stood and held out her tablet. "Is this your marriage contract to Ian?"

Jane took it and looked down at a photograph of a document she'd known all to well. She scrolled down and saw her father's signature and nodded. "This is it, but where did you find it? My father and Ian were the only two who had copies of it."

"It was folded up in the pages of one of her journals from that year," Neferu told her. "Along with this." Neferu swiped the image on the tablet and there was a picture of an open journal. "Read it out loud."

"Master Farrington visited me this evening, seeking my

counsel on the marriage of his daughter. I asked to speak to the young witchling but was denied that honor. The stones have told me that Jane Farrington is special. How special, I do not know and may never know.

"When I read the copy of the contract for marriage Farrington handed to me I was filled with cold dread. The feeling of evil washed over me as I read the contract giving away Jane's power to young Ian. A voice I'd never heard washed over me, warning of the story of the Selkie. I told Farrington the contract was cursed. That Ian was a Selkie— a person using his handsome appearance to disguise what's underneath. I saw underneath Ian's disguise and nothing but heartbreak and evil resides there. He must be cast out of the Tenebris or their future is lost." Jane took a breath and read on. She was so engrossed in the story she couldn't stop reading.

"Farrington nodded and thanked me. He left, and as I said farewell I learned two things. The first was that Farrington would condemn his daughter to a sad fate for I saw how the next four hundred years would play out. The young witch would be alone, running for her life.

"The second vision occurred when I looked into the circle and saw the young witch standing with her mother. A light shown upon her and I swore I saw my husband standing next to her with his hand in hers as he looked lovingly down upon her. Only, it was my husband as a young man, not the older man he is now becoming. I know in my heart of hearts that Jane Farrington is somehow linked to my family."

Jane read the last word and looked up. Everyone was staring at her as her mind and her magic swirled. "My father lied and defied the stone keeper. I never should have been engaged to Ian."

"Stone keepers follow the same laws of love as witches. True love makes it possible for you to have children. True love grants you tremendous power as you join into one," Zoey said in wonder as Jane flipped the images until she saw a picture of the last journal entry.

"Mariam saw Galen and me in the circle the night my father visited. It wasn't her husband looking at me, it was *Galen*." Jane's heart beat madly, and it felt as if her magic were cheering. "Oh my Goddess, Galen is my true love."

Zoey clapped her hands and Polly looked as if she were going to cry.

"We need to tell Galen," Slade said suddenly.

Jane cringed. "I don't know how he'll take it. I'm excited I found my true love. I know they're hard to find and even harder to recognize sometimes. What if he doesn't recognize it and leaves, thinking we're all crazy?"

"He's already showing signs of a true love bond. He won't leave you." Slade sounded so sure of it that Jane let her hopes soar. "Plus, if we have to battle Ian, true love will give you greater powers. No one will protect you more than your true love," Slade told her before looking lovingly at Zoey.

"That goes both ways. My powers are stronger when I protect my love. Not only that, but I think the bond had strengthened my powers in general," Zoey told her as she held Slade's hand in hers.

Linus cleared his throat and drew everyone's attention. "We know Ian's already here. He'll be coming for our Jane. I vote we tell Galen everything. Now."

Suddenly it was done. The council voted and Galen would be brought into Jane's battle.

"I don't even know how to tell him," Jane admitted.

Linus shook his head. "True love should be explained by

someone who knows it. Intimately. The only man here who does is Slade."

"You want me to tell Galen about his family history and oh, by the way, the girl you like is actually your true love and you'll now live for five thousand years taking care of witches and the stones back in Scotland?" Slade asked without a hint of expression.

"Exactly. I knew you were the right man for the job, son." Linus thumped Slade on the back as he walked by him and opened the front door. "No time like the present."

Slade kissed Zoey and held out his hand to Neferu who handed him the tablet. The door closed behind him and Zoey burst out laughing. "I would give anything to witness that talk. You know, I could cast that invisibility spell . . ."

"Don't even think about it," Lauren said as she placed her hands on her hips. "Your wedding is just over two weeks away. We have a seating chart to go over. We have a first dance to pick out. We need to finalize the flowers for your bouquet."

Zoey groaned and Jane smiled. The talk of wedding plans helped calm her as she thought about Galen and if he'd accept her or reject her.

14

"So, what seems to be the matter today?" Galen asked as he looked up from the chart Slade filled out. Nothing looked wrong. "Or do you need a physical?"

"No, I am in perfect health and will be for many centuries to come."

"Um, okay. Then what can I do to help you?" Galen took a seat on the rolling stool in his exam room and faced Slade.

"I've been sent to talk to you as I'm the only male with a true love mate." Galen opened his mouth but nothing came out. He had no idea what Slade was talking about as the huge man shifted uncomfortably in the plastic chair. "See, when a man and woman love each other—"

"Okay, Slade. I have patients to see. I know about sex, I learned all about it even before medical school. I don't know why you thought I needed to know this, but rest assured I do."

"Shut up and sit down," Slade snapped with frustration. "This has nothing to do with sex and you might as well cancel your other appointments. This is going to blow your little human mind. And until you accept what I tell you, you are still just a human."

Galen felt his jaw tighten as he tried to keep his cool. "You see, I'm a human and you're a human," he said sarcastically. He thought it might make Slade mad, but instead he laughed.

"I'm sorry. Here's the thing: what I'm about to tell you is going to make you open your mind to truths you didn't think were possible and it all goes back to two women that you love. Your Nan and Jane."

"Jane and I just met. Wait, what does my Nan have to do with this?"

"Your Nan and your grandfather were keepers of the Stones of Stenness and lived to be five thousand years old. You father is four thousand, nine hundred and eighty years old but didn't want the job so your Nan asked the Goddess what to do. She told your Nan that you and Jane, since she's your one true love, are now the keepers of the stones and advisors to the witches for the next five thousand years."

Galen's lips thinned as he pressed them tightly together and then he got it. "Oh, okay, you're here for a psych evaluation." Galen stood up. "Let me get some paperwork."

Slade lifted his hand and with the slight movement of one finger Galen was floating in the air until he was very carefully seated back on his stool.

"Maybe *I* need a psych eval because that's not possible."

"I'm a witch. Heck, most of the people in town are witches since the council moved here after Zoey ended Alexander's evil reign. Now, sit there and listen to a story of a man and woman who fell in love with each other almost five thousand years ago."

· · ·

GALEN STARED at the tablet Slade handed him after telling him the most far-fetched story of his grandparents, witches, and a war that had just ended. However, as he stared at the journal entry in his Nan's handwriting, dated over four hundred years before, he didn't quite know what to think.

"You're telling me the man my Nan warned Jane's father about, four hundred and some years ago, is the Ian from Jane's nightmares and he was Alexander's second-in-command and is now after Jane to enforce this marriage contract so he can gain enough power to take control of the Claritase and Tenebris?"

"Yes!" Slade said, flopping back in his chair in relief. "Finally. You get it."

"You think as soon as I find my true love, who you all think is Jane, that the two of us will take over as stone keepers on Orkney to help usher in a new age of witches by offering advice and providing a safe place for them to come and recharge?"

Slade nodded. "And commune with the Goddess."

"And the Goddess is who invented witches to help humans as they started to populate Earth?"

Slade nodded again. "You could say the stone keepers are witch doctors. They look after witches' magical wellbeing."

Galen was quiet as he looked at the pictures on the tablet for the tenth time. This just couldn't be. "Yeah, I don't believe it. Sorry. I don't know what parlor trick you did to make me think I was floating—" Slade grabbed his hand and the next thing Galen knew they were in the middle of the Standing Stones of Stenness. "Oh my God."

"Goddess," Slade corrected automatically. "Believe me now?"

Slade looked around the place he'd spent visiting every

summer. His Nan had taught him old traditional songs along with the history of the stones. "Nan told me stories about how she thought the stones were a gift from the Goddess. She said one night right after my umpteen great-grandfather was born a beautiful woman named Celesta visited. She brought them out here and showed them the stones that hadn't been there just an hour before. She told them they were to be the protectors of the stones and all the secrets that came with it. I'm guessing you all are the secrets and that those weren't my ancestors, but my actual Nan and Grandfather."

Slade nodded. "That's right. Celesta was the first Grand Mistress appointed by the Goddess herself."

"Can I go into the cottage?" Galen asked after a moment. He needed to be inside. He needed to feel Nan's presence.

"If you can. So far no other keeper has been able to enter it," Slade told him as they walked through the cold, clear Scottish night and down the hill to Sinclair Cottage. It might have been a cottage five thousand years before . . . well, probably a hut, but then it had become a cottage and now it resembled a large stone manor house.

Galen bent down and counted out the rocks. He lifted the one he was looking for and picked up the key. He slid it into the lock and then he walked inside. He flipped on the lights, grateful that they turned on. The house still smelled of his Nan even after two years. He turned back around and looked out the front door just as his Nan had done. There, up in the middle of the stones, he saw himself with Jane. Tears pressed against his eyes as he watched a golden vision of himself place a hand on Jane's swollen abdomen.

"How did you know Jane's my true love?" Galen asked as the vision faded.

"You love her, right?"

Galen nodded. "I shouldn't so soon. It's not rational." He paused and then laughed. "Then again, none of this is rational."

"Did you ever find it strange that Zoey and I have the exact same color of eyes? Lavender of all colors. It's not exactly common, yet we both have it."

"I had noticed that. I figured it was contacts."

Slade shook his head. "Our powers recognize our true loves. When our hearts and our minds accept that we love that person, and if they love you as well, you bond. Your eyes show it so all can see that you're bonded. After all, your eyes are the windows to your soul. A true love means two souls have become one. With witches, our eye color becomes the manifestation of the combination of powers. If you have water power, you have deep blue eyes. If your true love has earth powers, or green eyes, then you both end up with teal eyes. A fire witch will have reddish eyes and so on."

"But I'm not a witch," Galen pointed out.

"No, but your family has been blessed by the Goddess. Go look at your eyes."

Galen walked over to the mirror in the formal sitting room as he remembered telling Jane about the beautiful gold flecks in her eyes. He looked and at first glance saw nothing. Then he leaned closer and froze. "I have gold flecks in my eyes. They look like sparks. I've never had those before. What happened to my eyes?"

"You bonded with Jane. She has the same gold flecks."

"The vision I saw of Jane and me up at the stones were comprised of gold dust." Galen couldn't look away from his eyes. "If this is all true, what happens now?"

"I call everyone here. You tell Jane how you feel. Then you'll read this letter from your Nan," Slade said, walking over to the thick envelope lying in the middle of the kitchen table.

"By doing all this, I will be protecting Jane?"

"I don't know for sure. You have an overwhelming desire to protect each other and you have a bond that makes you unbreakable. It seems it will have an effect on the threat Ian poses. But Galen, as the stone keeper you will no longer be the doctor in Moonshine. You and Jane will be here. Witches will flock here as soon as it's known there's a new stone keeper. Especially since Alexander is dead. They've needed the healing powers of the stones that have been denied to them for far too long."

Galen wanted to argue, but took a deep breath to settle himself and the most amazing feeling of rightness enveloped him. "Call everyone here."

15

Jane's heart pounded as every witch in Moonshine Hollow and what seemed like the whole world *poofed* into the middle of the standing stones. Zoey held her hand as they traveled together after receiving the text from Slade.

Witches from all over the world were arriving every second. There were gasps of pleasure, surprise, and hope. Jane could feel it in the air as the entire hilltop filled with witches. There were witches who had been in hiding for centuries just as Jane herself had been. She felt an instant connection to them as witches embraced and tears were shed.

"Jane!"

Jane looked down toward a beautiful manor house. With a wiggle of her fingers, the night was lit up by hundreds of brightly colored lanterns floating above them. Galen ran toward her and she was instantly running toward him. Galen opened his arms and then she was in them.

"I can't believe this is all real. Slade has told me about so much, but one thing he didn't need to tell me was that I love you. I already knew that."

"Oh, Galen! I love you too." Jane looked into his eyes, and the gold flecks in them seemed to move to show her their future.

"I know this is crazy, Jane, but I have never felt so sure about anything in my entire life. This is where I'm supposed to be and nothing would make me happier than if you are here with me."

Jane laughed as she held his hands in hers. "On one condition."

"Anything."

"Marry me right now," she said with the biggest smile. She'd seen a vision in his eyes. A marriage, a battle, and then happiness. Jane glanced behind her and saw Zoey nod at her. It was the vision she'd seen as well.

"I wouldn't have been able to wait." Galen lowered his lips to hers and then it was if they were all alone. Jane's whole world was centered on where their lips met.

"We've never had a stone keeper's wedding before," Jane finally heard Linus mutter.

"It's nothing we can't handle," Lauren answered and Jane was pretty sure the Grand Mistress was wiping a tear from her eye. "Slade, you and Samuel get Galen ready. Zoey and Polly, you get Jane ready. Leave everything else up to us."

IT TOOK five hundred witches less than five minutes to put a dream wedding into motion. From her spot inside the master bedroom of the Sinclair Cottage, Jane heard the sound of harps playing up at the stones.

Jane wore a long-sleeved white velvet dress that she'd used her powers to create. "What do I do now?"

"You marry the man you love," Zoey said before hugging her tightly. "I knew you'd have happiness."

"There's a battle yet to come," Jane warned.

"I know. We aren't to worry about it today. Today we have hope."

"It's time. The sun is about to rise," Polly said gently.

The three walked from the bedroom and out the open front door. Jane gasped as she saw all the women lining the path from the door to the stones.

"For the stone keeper," an older woman who looked very much like Jane's mother stood with two younger women behind her and Fern alongside her spoke to Jane. "And for my niece," she said with a sniffle as she handed a bloom to Jane. "The flower of our Langley family for your bouquet."

Her aunt! And she had more cousins. Jane reached for her and pulled them into an embrace. "I can't wait to spend time together."

"For the stone keeper. The flower of our family." The next woman in line said as her family bowed and handed another beautiful bloom to the bride.

And on and on it went as Jane walked behind Zoey and Polly toward the stones. Galen stood next to the grand master and grand mistress with Slade and Samuel standing slightly behind him. Their eyes were glued to Zoey and Polly. Jane smiled at the thought of more witch weddings. This was hope. This was their future beginning to unfold.

GALEN WATCHED as a vision in white velvet seemed to float toward him, leaving behind a path of golden dust that glowed in the sunlight. They were all winging the ceremony, but a love unlike anything he'd felt filled him from the large group in attendance.

"Son." Galen spun around and there stood Niles and Neferu with his parents.

"Dad! Mom!"

His father wrapped him tightly in a hug. "I'm sorry. I wasn't strong enough to sacrifice myself to fulfill our family's duty."

"I don't think you were meant to. I think it was always supposed to be me. I don't know how I know that, but I know it."

His mother hugged him first as she dabbed at the tears. "This is all so new to me, but it makes sense. I knew you were special the moment you were born."

Then his father hugged him one last time before turning to Linus. "I remember you, Grand Master. You often came here to meditate when I was younger."

"I remember you too. It's good to see you again. You must be very proud of your son."

"I am and I always have been. I'm also here to join you in the ceremony. My mother left me with instructions."

"Oh thank Goddess, because we don't know what we're doing," Grand Mistress Lauren whispered and everyone laughed. But then the laughter faded as Jane approached them. Magnus, Zoey's father, handed Zoey a flower, then Jane accepted a flower from Polly and finally the last flower from Zoey.

Jane held an explosion of color in her hands as flowers in all shapes, sizes, and colors seemed to cascade naturally, forming the bridal bouquet.

Galen was at her side, and the ceremony started as the sun rose. From the center of the standing stones, they pledged their love to each other. The grand mistress and the grand master blessed them, then his father stepped forward.

"As the eldest Sinclair, I hereby renounce any claim to

the stones or powers given to me by the Goddess and ask that all the Sinclair powers be vested into the couple before us now. True love and destiny have given us two new keepers. One with witch's blood and one with the keeper's blood. Together their guidance, love, and strength will be a beacon for all witches to unite once again. With the powers imbued in my family by the Goddess herself and from Grand Mistress Celesta, I now pronounce Galen and Jane Sinclair husband and wife *and* the Stone Keepers of Stenness. My son, you may kiss your bride."

Galen looked down at his bride's face awash in the golden glow of the rising sun and pledged his life to her while thanking the Goddess for such a gift. He lowered his lips, and when they brushed against Jane's, a golden burst of light shot out like a halo, rising above the stones to surround all in attendance. Galen would have sworn in that moment he felt their souls become one.

Zoey watched the ceremony with her heart full of hope. She knew what was ahead of them. The visions of what was to come were becoming stronger. Ian would make his move soon. But this morning . . . this morning there was happiness and hope for a future that hadn't been there for centuries.

"That will be us soon, sweetness," Slade whispered to her as he placed his hand at her hip and pulled her tightly against his side.

"Something bad is going to happen soon," Zoey told him as she leaned against him for strength.

"I've been talking to your father about it. What if we make it on our terms?"

"What do you mean?" Zoey asked as she pulled away from him to look up at Slade.

"Ian wants Jane, so let's set a trap."

Zoey looked out at the crowd gathered around the ancient standing stones. A whole generation of centuries-old men and women looked as if they were at a middle school dance. Single men were huddled on one side scoping out the single women on the other side, and the single women were staring at the single men in both awe and a little bit of trepidation. Before a new generation of witches could be born, Zoey and Slade had to show the way with the first Claritase and Tenebris wedding. And before she could enjoy her wedding, she needed Ian taken care of.

"Did you tell her about our plan?" Zoey's father asked Slade as he, Linus, and Lauren joined them.

"I was just about to." Slade didn't let go of her as he looked down at her. His eyes conveyed everything about this plan. It was dangerous, but he'd protect her with his life. But he knew that promise went both ways.

"What's the plan?"

"Ian wants Jane, but he won't come into town to get her. I say we set it up so he thinks he has her all to himself when in reality we'll have him surrounded," Slade told the group.

"How do you plan on doing that?" Lauren asked.

"We take a page from Ian's book and spell some humans into tipping him off."

"I've been working on my powers. I can do that. I can also create a thunderstorm to provide us with cover. The rain and the electricity in the air will help hide us."

Zoey turned to her dad with surprise. "You can do that?"

Grand Master Linus nodded. "You two are the most powerful witches we've had in millennia. Magnus has far exceeded our expectations and is developing powers and abilities that were only theoretical until now. And he's mastering them. Your father will do great things for the people of this world, both witches and humans."

Zoey wrapped her arms around her father and hugged him tight. "I'm so proud of you."

"I'm proud of you too, Jellybean. I love nothing more than spending time with you. I'm thankful everyday that you forgave me for leaving when you were younger."

"And you'll love nothing more than holding your grandchild, isn't that right?" Lauren asked with a wink.

"You're worse than my mother." Zoey laughed but Lauren seemed to take that as a compliment.

"Just imagine, Linus. A baby witchling," Lauren happily sighed.

Zoey reached out and grabbed Lauren and Linus by their hands as they teared up. She froze. Images flashed in front of her. Pain. Defeat. Death.

She yanked her hands away as if scorched and tried to put on a smile. Tonight would be the last happy night they'd all have together.

16

THE CELEBRATION of Jane and Galen's marriage lasted all day. Every family came to introduce themselves to the happy couple. Stone keepers from other sites around the world all offered assistance should they need it. The witches started *poofing* home as the party wound down with excited promises to all gather again soon for the first Claritase and Tenebris marriage. Eventually it was just Jane, Galen, and their Moonshine Hollow friends who were left.

"Goodnight, my dears," Lauren said, kissing them on their cheeks. "Tonight is yours but tomorrow we must put an end to this threat once and for all. May the Goddess bless you both."

Jane and Galen said their goodbyes and then it was just the two of them. Galen picked her up and carried her over the threshold and into their new life together as husband and wife.

BACK IN MOONSHINE HOLLOW, the wedding seemed like a lifetime ago as they all crammed into Zoey and Slade's house. "No way," Galen practically shouted when Slade finished telling them his plan to use Jane for bait.

"I think it's a good idea. Why live in fear waiting for him to make his move when we can do it on our terms with our entire team present?" Jane told him. She placed her hand on his and squeezed it. "I've waited over four hundred years to be rid of Ian and I'm tired of waiting. I'm tired of not living my life. I'm tired of living in fear. I'm done putting my life on hold for Ian. I've found love and a new purpose in my life and I can't wait to get started."

"Then I'm coming with you," Galen demanded.

"You can come with me. We'll be very close to her so you can get to her immediately if you need to," Slade said in such a way it left Galen very little room to argue.

"How are you going to get me alone and have Ian know about it?" Jane asked after Galen nodded his head in agreement to Slade's plan.

"The walking bridge over Earnest Creek. You can look down on it from the lookout you created on the mountain. Plus, there's enough forest cover on both sides of the creek for plenty of us to hide," Slade told her. "Magnus will start a storm at nightfall. You will need to close the bridge. During the day Magnus will spell humans to walk around the woods talking about you closing the bridge all by yourself and how dangerous it is. Ian will come. He won't be able to stop himself, thinking that he has you trapped."

"When?" Jane asked after taking a deep breath.

"Tonight," Magnus answered. "If you agree, I'll put everything into motion while you are at work. It's going to be a nice day today and the forest will be packed with hikers. I want you warning everyone that while the bridge is open now, you will be closing it tonight for the foreseeable future due to the anticipated thunderstorms. Can you do that?"

Jane nodded. "Let's do this."

Magnus leaned over and hugged her. "You'll be fine. I know because my daughter told me so."

"Then I know this will work. I'll see you all tonight."

Galen stood and together he and Jane walked from Zoey's house hand in hand. She had an evil witch to show that she wasn't going to be pushed around anymore.

ZOEY SWALLOWED hard as her house began to empty out. "Wait," she said when just Slade, her father, Vilma, and Agnes were left. "I had a vision about tonight and someone dies."

"Could you tell who?" Vilma asked.

Zoey shook her head. Her heart was breaking in two. She'd been beating herself up trying to figure out who it was. "I got it when I touched Lauren and Linus yesterday."

Agnes sighed. "I'm sorry, but it could be anyone under them. As you know the Grand Master and Grand Mistress get their power from their people and you could be picking up anyone's future."

"Did you get the feeling you could stop it?" Vilma asked her and it seemed she already knew what Zoey was going to say.

"No. That's what's killing me. I can't see who it is, and I can't stop it. I know I can't." Zoey fought back tears. "Because what accompanied the vision was a feeling of such heartbreak I knew it would be true no matter what I did."

The room was solemn as they listened to her tell them of her vision.

"All we can do is protect each other. If the Goddess calls

any one of us home, we must go," her father said to her as he cupped her face with his hands and kissed her forehead just as he'd done when she was a child. "I'm going to set things in motion. Be safe, Jellybean."

Agnes handed her a power shake. "Drink this right before tonight. It'll help."

Vilma hugged her tight. "It's not your fault if someone dies, Zoey. Maybe it's Ian who dies. Your visions don't make you responsible for them."

Zoey nodded but as they left she knew someone she cared about wasn't coming home from the fight.

JANE TRIED to go about her day as if nothing out of the ordinary was happening. It was probably her imagination, but she felt as if she could feel Ian's eyes on her. She stood outside of her office calling out to people to enjoy the nice day while it lasted. The sun was out and people were filling the hiking trails to enjoy the practically spring like day in December.

"I'm closing the bridge tonight since we have a storm warning. Make sure you're back by nightfall!" Jane shouted out to every new group of hikers.

Witches were already in position near the bridge. Galen was with them, but even knowing there were at least five witches within a hundred feet of her, Jane still felt jumpy.

Jane couldn't tell if it happened too fast or too slow, but the sun began to set and people began to leave. As darkness fell, the last car pulled out of the lot and the wind began to pick up. It was time.

. . .

ZOEY STOOD next to her father at the lookout on Earnest Mountain. He held up his hands and his eyed glazed over as he pulled energy from the heavens. Storm clouds built, thunder rolled, the wind picked up, and blue lightning streaked across the night sky.

Zoey watched in awe, as did every other witch around them.

"He's here," Slade said as he pointed to the figure approaching the bridge. Jane was pretending to close it as Ian pushed back his hoodie and smirked at her back, thinking he'd ambushed her.

In a blink of Zoey's eye, they were all within ten feet of Ian, undetected under the cover of the storm. Jane stood and as she slowly turned to face him, Zoey saw the determination in her face.

"Do you feel that?" Zoey whispered frantically.

Linus and Lauren nodded. No one else did though.

"We're not alone," Linus said.

"It's an evil unlike any I've ever felt," Lauren whispered. "Even worse than Alexander."

"Is it Ian? Has he grown that strong?" Slade asked.

"I don't think so," Linus said as he and Lauren looked at each other.

"Slade, Zoey, take care of Jane and end Ian. We'll be back," Lauren ordered.

Zoey nodded as she continued to look around. "I don't know what it is, but it's foul. A stench of decay that seems to be sticking to everything around us."

"I don't care what it is, you swore to protect Jane!" Galen whispered harshly.

"And I will," Zoey swore.

"Then kill him!"

Zoey shook her head. "I'm sorry, Galen. Jane made me

promise not to step in until she has her say. She wants to handle Ian. It's her right after everything he's put her through. Don't worry. There are people all around to help her. No harm will come to her."

Zoey took one last glance around as Ian made his move. Now she had a promise to keep and couldn't be distracted.

17

"I'VE BEEN WAITING FOR YOU."

Jane looked up from where she'd been pretending to mess with the lock on the bridge's gate and slowly turned around. "Ian!" Jane almost laughed at how pleased he seemed to be for supposedly catching her off guard.

"My dear betrothed," he called out over the rising winds. "I have one final proposal for you."

"You never proposed the first time," Jane pointed out as she turned fully to face him. She was done running. One of them wasn't going to make it out of the woods that night, and it wasn't going to be her.

"Then take this proposal as the only one you'll ever get. Option one: Marry me and give me your powers—all of them. I've waited too long and you owe them to me. You do that and I'll let you live. Or—" Ian smiled evilly, "—option two, I take your powers and kill you where you stand."

"Hmm." Jane called her powers to her, ready for action. She felt the power of the earth rising from the soles of her feet and racing toward her fingers. "I'll go with option three."

"You never were the brightest, Jane. I was never marrying you for your smarts, though. I just want your powers. The ones no one ever taught you to use. Wasn't that nice of your father?"

"If I'm not that smart, how have I evaded you for four hundred years? Gee Ian, what does that say about you?"

Red sparks sputtered in the rain around Ian as he tried to control his anger. "Option one or two, which one is it to be Jane?"

Jane took a deep breath and planted her feet wide. "Option three."

"There is no—"

Jane raised her hands and let her powers burst free. The first hit knocked Ian back several feet as he tried to block her power. "I will never be under your control, Ian!" Jane yelled as she drew power from the trees, the plants, the grass, and the very earth itself. "No longer do you have any claim to me. I am done being afraid of you!"

The storm suddenly stopped, and as the clouds parted, the moon shown down on the battle. Ian was strong. Strong enough that Jane questioned her power. But then she saw Galen and felt his power of determination. She saw Slade, Zoey, Polly, and Neferu. She felt witches moving into place all around them until they were fully encircled.

"We are here for you," Jane heard Magnus say calmly behind her as Ian began to look about frantically.

"What are the chances of all of us meeting you here?" Slade asked from directly behind Ian. They were cousins, and while Jane had a strong reason to hate Ian, so did Slade.

The moment of surprise cost Ian as it gave Jane the chance to hit him with a power burst. Ian dropped to his knees. Blood poured from his nose and ears as he depleted more and more of his power.

"You're taking my powers and will become just like me," he accused.

"I'm showing you that you lost. I'm showing you I have always been stronger than you. And I'm showing you that your reign of terror is at an end. But I'm not going to take your powers. No one wants powers tainted with evil. Good bye, Ian."

Jane looked up at Zoey and nodded.

ZOEY CONCENTRATED her powers into the palm of her hand. As the fifth element she had the power to simply end life and send it into a void of nothingness. When Jane nodded at her, Zoey sent the white light flying at Ian. It looked like a halo of light circling around a black center. When it hit Ian he simply disappeared into nothingness, his evil powers along with him.

"*No!*" A booming voice echoed through the valley as the clouds reformed and opened up again. Zoey felt the warmth of rain on her body as people began to scream. They weren't being deluged with rain, but with blood.

Blood showered down on them as she looked around for the source of the voice. It hadn't been Ian. Ian was already gone.

The smell of rotting flesh filled the air as the blood rain covered them all. Slade wrapped a protective arm around her, but she shook him off. Her powers of protection were in full control.

"Polly, Samuel, take Galen and Jane to the safe house. Now!" Zoey yelled before turning to Slade. "Where are Linus and Lauren?"

"I don't know, but we have to protect our people."

Zoey and Slade began issuing orders. As she scanned

the area, blood ran in rivulets down her face. She wiped it away as she saw Jane with Galen, Polly, and Samuel. "Zoey!" Jane yelled.

"Go!" Zoey yelled back and even as Jane fought, Polly placed her hand on hers and then they were gone.

"Did you do this?" Zoey yelled over the thunder at her father.

"No!" he paused and looked up river. "Zoey, look!"

Zoey turned and saw a tsunami of blood rushing down the creek straight for them. "Everyone out. Now!"

Zoey and Slade issued the order and the witches were only too happy to comply.

"I haven't seen such black magic since the evil of Apep in ancient Egypt," Neferu screamed. Zoey turned to see the woman was completely covered in blood.

"Get out of here," Zoey yelled.

"Not without Lauren and Linus."

"They're not here," Zoey told her as Slade grabbed her hand.

Zoey.

"Wait!" Zoey closed her eyes and heard it again. "I hear them."

Her father kissed her and then ran for the bridge.

"Dad, no!"

Blue light, neither the color of air nor the color of the water shot from his fingers and straight into the swelling red wave that was swallowing up trees, boulders, and everything in its path.

"Find them!" Zoey yelled at Slade and Neferu. "I can hear someone calling me."

They each ran in a different direction. Zoey closed her eyes and opened her senses.

Zoey.

She ran toward the voice, finding that when she climbed higher the voice got louder.

"Here!" she yelled over her shoulder as raced up a small path. Above her was a rock overhang. "Slade, Neferu, here!"

Zoey glanced back at her father once more. He was holding the giant wave back in a effort that left him shaking. Even from here she could see his arms shaking from the strain.

She heard Slade yell and then she heard him helping Neferu up the steep mountainside. Zoey reached up, dug her blood covered fingers into the crevasse of the overhang and pulled herself up.

"Zoey!"

"Grand mistress!" Zoey screamed as she dragged her body onto the top of the rock. "Linus!"

Zoey looked down as blood poured from Linus's body. The way Lauren was pressing her hands against his chest and her ashen face, Zoey knew it wasn't the blood rain, but Linus's own blood that was pooling on the rock under him.

"Take him to the clinic."

Lauren shook her head "I'm using all my power to keep him alive." Her tears flowed freely and converged with the blood rain until they dripped from her nose and cheeks.

Zoey spun around and looked down at Neferu and Slade. "Neferu, get Galen and meet us in the clinic now!" Neferu must have seen the look on Zoey's face because she *poofed* away instantly. "Slade, go to my dad and when you see my signal, I want you to get him to the clinic too."

Having a visual on the bridge, Slade disappeared a second later and *poofed* next to her father. Slade placed a hand on her father's shoulder and looked over at the ridge he knew she was on.

"Zoey, hurry." Lauren shook, her whole body looking as if she were going to pass out.

Zoey reached a hand to Lauren and with the other hand shot a bolt of white energy up into the sky a second before she lowered her hand to Linus and transported them.

18

SLADE SAW the burst of white light in the sky. "Time to go, sir," he yelled into Magnus's ear. The sound of his power battling with the churning blood wave was nearly deafening. Slade had them in the clinic as soon as Magnus nodded and broke off his defensive barrage of power.

What met Slade was worse than what he'd anticipated. Galen was pulling back the torn edges of Linus's sweater. Grand Mistress Lauren looked near death. Zoey's hands were over Linus's heart as she worked to save him with magic.

Silent tears ran down Neferu's face as witches began to fill the waiting room. News traveled fast.

"Galen, do something!" Zoey yelled. Slade and Magnus stepped closer as he saw that Zoey's hands were literally holding Linus's heart that was encased in a black oil-like substance. Her white power glowed around the organ helping it beat.

Galen's hands dropped as Slade got the full view. There was a slight shake of Galen's head that told Slade what they already knew.

"Son," Linus murmured. The barely whispered words could be heard as if he were screaming since everyone surrounding him was shocked and silent.

Slade rushed forward and took Linus's hand as Galen stepped back and wrapped one arm around Lauren and the other around Jane.

"In all ways that matter, you are my son and I'm so proud of the man you've become."

Slade shook his head. "I'm the man I am because of you. Only because of you. You believed in me when no on else did. I love you."

"I knew you were special when you saved Magnus. And you're not done saving people. Magnus, come here."

Zoey's father came forward to stand next to Slade.

"You two are the future of the Tenebris. Magnus will lead you all into the future as your new grand master, for I've felt the power of the Goddess inside of him. Slade and Zoey will make sure there's a future to be led into. The greatest battle is yet to come. What attacked me is pure black magic and *must* be defeated. There *will* be happiness. There *will* be love. There *will* be new life. You must go forward together—Tenebris and Claritase. You must allow the Goddess to share these gifts even when the darkness comes. That is how you will win."

"No," Slade said strongly. "We can save you. Zoey can save you."

"The Goddess herself is welcoming me, son. It's my destiny." Linus smiled calmly at Slade.

Slade felt Linus's hand tighten on his as Zoey's white light began to dim around his heart. It was like the black substance was choking the life from him. "Helena is here with the Goddess. They all are. Ah, it's so beautiful."

"Mom," Slade said with surprise.

"She's as proud of you as I am. She always knew you were filled with goodness. She says now is the time to embrace it. Embrace everything you feel flowing inside and let your powers free. The Goddess agrees. We'll be watching and loving each and every one of you as you start the rebirth of the Tenebris and the Claritase. The world needs kindness. It needs goodness. It needs healing. And you, my dear witches, will heal the world even as you fight for your existence. Just don't forget—together. Live together. Love together. Stand together."

Linus squeezed Slade's hand one last time.

His hand went limp in Slade's grasp. Zoey's light went out around his heart. Lauren cried out, dropping to her knees praying to the Goddess to bring her friend back to her.

Niles and Raiden came forward silently. With a wave of Niles's fingers, a bowl of warm water and several cloths appeared.

Slade had to pull Zoey from where she collapsed over Linus, weeping. "I should have been able to save him."

"As powerful as you are my love, you're not more powerful than the Goddess. She called him home. Take care of your grand mistress. We'll prepare Linus's body for his return to the Goddess."

Zoey nodded sadly as she turned to find Neferu with her hand on Lauren's shoulder. Tears streamed down their faces as Zoey joined them.

"Together," Zoey said, repeating the prophecy Linus left for them.

Hand in hand, the women walked from the room and the door closed.

"His service needs to be at the stones," Galen said, as he

picked up a cloth and began helping the Tenebris council wipe the blood from Linus's body.

One by one, each councilmember bowed their head in agreement as they prepared for a funeral.

IT SEEMED a lifetime ago they'd gathered as Tenebris and Claritase for the first time in centuries for a wedding. But there they were, less than a day later, in the dark side of the morning at the Standing Stones of Stenness.

Linus had been dressed in a white robe and lay on a large table in the center of the stones. Tenebris and Claritase came from all over the world to place a flower or a candle around the body of the grand master.

Magnus had refused to be voted into the position until after the ceremony, but he stood at the head of the table with Grand Mistress Lauren as the people mourned the loss of their beloved leader.

Slade stood off to the side with the council of both the Tenebris and the Claritase. In the past, they had stood apart. Now they stood together. Zoey slipped her hand into his as they stood for hours as respects were paid.

Then as the sun began to break the horizon and shine onto Linus, the Goddess took his body, leaving behind only memories of him.

Magnus was voted as new Grand Master when Slade cast the final vote.

"On such a day, I am both saddened and honored by this gift." Magnus said to his people. "This goes against history, but as Grand Master Linus told us in his last words, we are forging a new future. As such, I name Slade as my Vice Master. He will be second-in-command and upon your vote of approval today will automatically fill the role of grand master should I not be able to until a vote can be held."

"I second!" Samuel called out loudly.

"Then we vote on the new position of Vice Master."

In short order, not only was Slade now second-in-command, Grand Mistress Lauren surprised everyone by holding her own vote naming Zoey her Vice Mistress.

After the cheers of support for Slade and Zoey quieted, Grand Master Magnus continued. "I will do everything in my power to carry out Grand Master Linus's last wishes. At the solstice, you are all invited here for the first witch marriage in four hundred years. For here we will hold the ceremony of my daughter's wedding to the man I have just named as my second-in-charge, but now get to call son. A human ceremony and reception will follow immediately after in Moonshine Hollow. I hope you will join Grand Mistress Lauren and me at that as well."

"We look forward to attending many more such love unions between our people," Grand Mistress Lauren told the crowd. "To honor such a blessing as the true love bond, Grand Master Magnus and I will attend every wedding as we prepare schools all over the witch communities in the hopes of a very prosperous future of little witchlings and the next generation of Tenebris and Claritase. A generation who will heed the Goddess's call to help all those in need."

Slade leaned down to his love's ear. "We could start on that if you'd like."

"You want little witchlings running around accidently spelling you?" Zoey asked with the first smile he'd seen on her face recently.

"I'd love nothing more."

"It's a good thing you're getting married soon then."

"Dad!" Zoey said full of embarrassment.

"I'll make you a special drink," Agnes said, joining them.

"Oh, your famous fertility drink. I'll make a special batch of moonshine to go with it," Vilma said with a nod of her head.

Slade smiled as he felt Zoey trying not to laugh. "You have fertility moonshine?"

"No, the normal moonshine does enough to get you frisky."

"Frisky, huh?" Polly asked and Slade saw her eyes go to Samuel.

"I think we might want to rethink the champagne at the wedding, Grand Mistress Lauren," Vilma said with a smile full of mischief. "My moonshine might really aid in togetherness. After all, it's what Grand Master Linus wanted."

Even with the shine of unshed tears in her eyes, Grand Mistress Lauren laughed and nodded. "I think that's a wonderful idea. I was so focused on it being a royal wedding. What it needs to be is a celebration—a celebration of life, love, and togetherness."

"Thank Goddess," Zoey called out. "Polly, we need to grab Jane and Maribelle and start wedding planning from scratch!" Zoey spun and kissed Slade before reaching out to grab Polly's hand. "We don't have a moment to lose."

As they *poofed* away, Slade turned to Grand Mistress Lauren. "Thank you."

"Don't thank me yet. My women have been in hiding for centuries. Your men have been too. We're going to move past this shyness in a big way. Vilma, I hope you can make a whole heap of that moonshine because I want some weddings and witchlings soon."

"No pressure, son." Slade's soon-to-be father-in-law

laughed as he slapped Slade's back. "But I expect many a little witchling, too."

Slade shook his head as he stood by the council's side and watched joy and hope begin to fill the stones. With death came life. And with Linus's death, new life was breathed into the Claritase and Tenebris. He listened as the witches began talks of healing once again. Talk of sharing love and compassion. Talks of helping the humans when they needed it most. It was truly magical.

EPILOGUE

ZOEY WALKED through the standing stones, escorted by her mother and stepfather as the sun began to set. In the center her true love stood waiting for her. While the wedding planning had taken on a party atmosphere, there were still some parts Zoey knew were important to her parents and to Grand Mistress Lauren—like Slade in a tuxedo.

Thank Goddess Lauren had insisted on it because Zoey had never seen such a sexy sight before. He stood tall and strong and with so much love in his eyes that she could see the lavender bond that connected their hearts together.

With Polly by her side and Samuel by Slade's, they stood in front of her father and Grand Mistress Lauren and pledged their love to each other.

Her father wrapped a cloth with Slade and Zoey's new family crest upon it around their joined hands. It was the first she'd seen it. It was a mix of the Rode family crest and Slade's mother's crest. Slade sucked in a breath as he looked down at it while her father spoke.

"I felt as if Linus would approve," Grand Mistress Lauren whispered.

Zoey looked to where Slade ran a finger over the bird flying with a laurel in his beak and knew that must be part of Linus's family crest.

Zoey smiled up at her love and then they were kissing. One hand slid against her cheek as the other wrapped around her waist and dipped her back. The kiss was far more than a peck. It was a promise of a lifetime of love.

SLADE DIPPED his wife back for a second time and kissed her. If she'd thought the first kiss at the stones was something, the second one in Moonshine had her seeing stars. At least that's what Slade hoped as all of Moonshine Hollow, the Tenebris, and the Claritase cheered.

Slade took his wife's hand, and after they were announced husband and wife, he stepped down and kissed his mother-in-law's cheek before shaking her husband's hand. In this ceremony, Magnus had escorted Zoey down the aisle as father of the bride. Slade shook his hand as Zoey hugged her father. Then they ran down the corridor of their cheering friends. Behind them, his best man, Samuel, held out his arm for Polly, who was the maid of honor. Former Moonshine sheriff, Luke Tanner escorted Maribelle. Galen escorted Jane as the wedding party joined the new husband and wife in the receiving line.

THE BARN, decorated with white and lavender, glowed. As Zoey and Slade walked hand in hand to join the reception, all they could hear, see, and feel was happiness.

"It's so nice to hear that," Zoey said with a happy smile.

"I wonder if the humans have any idea they're surrounded by witches," Slade joked.

"They might get an idea if Lauren keeps handing out that moonshine."

"Then we better not keep them waiting. Let's celebrate, sweetness."

"While we can."

Slade shook his head. "No, let's always celebrate our love. I know the worst is to come, but this . . . this is what we're fighting for."

Slade laced his hand with hers and together they walked into the reception. The band started up a slow song as Holt Everett, a country singer from Keeneston, Kentucky who was making a name for himself in the Nashville country scene, sang about love as Zoey and Slade shared their first dance.

As the song progressed, Zoey's mother and stepfather joined them. Magnus and Lauren stepped out next, followed by Galen and Jane, Maribelle and Dale, Luke and his girlfriend Ava from Keeneston, and all the other couples in Moonshine. The song ended and Slade kissed his wife to the cheers of their friends and family.

"A toast to the happy couple!" Grand Mistress called out as shot glasses of moonshine were passed around. "To Slade and Zoey."

"To Slade and Zoey!"

"A toast!" Grand Master Magnus called out as more rounds of shots were passed out. "May my beloved daughter live happily ever after with her true love."

"To happily ever after!" the crowd cheered and then drank.

The band picked a fast song and the dance floor filled with human couples.

"Come on, someone make a move," Grand Mistress Lauren muttered under her breath. Samuel stepped from one side of the dance floor and walked over to Polly. He held out his hand. When she took it, Grand Mistress Lauren gave Magnus a high five.

"It's starting something, look!" Magnus said excitedly as Raiden asked Fern to dance. Soon the dance floor was filled with human partners, witch partners, and even some human and witch dance partners.

Zoey laughed and shook her head at her father and Lauren. "You two are so bad."

Lauren suddenly looked every inch the grand mistress she was. "I am simply ensuring my people's happiness."

"And making sure you'll be invited to plenty of weddings and filling schools with witchlings," Slade mentioned.

"Oh look," Grand Mistress Lauren said. "I need to talk to Vilma and Agnes."

Zoey and Slade laughed as the grand mistress hurried off. With a flick of her hand, the back table was filled with more moonshine.

"My dear, you're beautiful. Go enjoy your reception," her father said to Zoey while he hugged her tight.

"You feel it, right? The disruption in the magic?" Zoey asked, her voice low so she wasn't overheard.

"Yes. But we are safe for now. Enjoy your honeymoon. I have a very special grandchild to meet."

"Not you, too," Zoey groaned.

Her father simply laughed and walked to join the others.

"Would my bride like a drink?" Slade asked.

"I'd love one. Then I'm going to make you dance all night long."

"I remember the last time I saw you dancing. It was the night we met. You were half-naked up on that stage shaking what the Goddess gave you. The night fate made her first move to making me the happiest man alive."

Zoey gasped and pretended to smack his arm. "I was not dancing on that stage! I was trying to rescue my client from strippers."

"As I recall, I rescued you from the strippers."

Zoey tried not to laugh as she looked at her husband. "I can't wait until I rescue you."

"You already have. Everyday you're with me. You rescue my heart from the lonely existence that was my life before you were in it."

"I love you." Zoey rose up on her toes and placed a kiss on his lips.

"I love you too."

Zoey wrapped her arms around Slade's neck as they danced to the music. For tonight they were happy, and for tonight the town of Moonshine Hollow was filled with nothing but love, happiness, and hope for the future.

THE END

Forever Devoted

Forever Hunted

Forever Guarded

Forever Notorious

Forever Ventured

Forever Freed

Forever Saved (coming July/August 2020)

Shadows Landing Series

Saving Shadows

Sunken Shadows

Lasting Shadows

Fierce Shadows

Broken Shadows (coming October 2020)

Women of Power Series

Chosen for Power

Built for Power

Fashioned for Power

Destined for Power

Web of Lies Series

Whispered Lies

Rogue Lies

Shattered Lies

Moonshine Hollow Series

Moonshine & Murder

Moonshine & Malice

Moonshine & Mayhem

Moonshine & Mischief

ABOUT THE AUTHOR

Kathleen Brooks is a New York Times, Wall Street Journal, and USA Today bestselling author. Kathleen's stories are romantic suspense featuring strong female heroines, humor, and happily-ever-afters. Her Bluegrass Series and follow-up Bluegrass Brothers Series feature small town charm with quirky characters that have captured the hearts of readers around the world.

Kathleen is an animal lover who supports rescue organizations and other non-profit organizations such as Friends and Vets Helping Pets whose goals are to protect and save our four-legged family members.

Email Notice of New Releases

https://kathleen-brooks.com/new-release-notifications

Kathleen's Website
www.kathleen-brooks.com
Facebook Page
www.facebook.com/KathleenBrooksAuthor
Twitter
www.twitter.com/BluegrassBrooks
Goodreads
www.goodreads.com